Keith Waterhouse

KU-606-283

Soho

SCEPTRE

First published in Great Britain in 2001 by Hodder & Stoughton

This edition published in 2014 by Sceptre
An imprint of Hodder & Stoughton
An Hachette UK company

2

Copyright © Keith Waterhouse 2001

The right of Keith Waterhouse to be identified as the Author
of the Work has been asserted by him in accordance with the
Copyright, Designs and Patents Act 1988.

All rights reserved. No part of this publication may be
reproduced, stored in a retrieval system, or transmitted, in any form
or by any means without the prior written permission of the publisher,
nor be otherwise circulated in any form of binding or cover other
than that in which it is published and without a similar condition
being imposed on the subsequent purchaser.

All characters in this publication are fictitious and any resemblance
to real persons, living or dead is purely coincidental.

A CIP catalogue record for this title is
available from the British Library

ISBN 978 1 444 75395 0

Typeset in Sabon MT by Palimpsest Book Production Limited,
Falkirk, Stirlingshire
Printed and bound in Great Britain by Clays Ltd, St Ives plc

Hodder & Stoughton policy is to use papers that are natural,
renewable and recyclable products and made from wood grown
in sustainable forests. The logging and manufacturing processes are
expected to conform to the environmental regulations of
the country of origin.

Hodder & Stoughton Ltd
338 Euston Road
London NW1 3BH

www.sceptrebooks.com

Author's Note

Since this is a work of fiction, I have permitted myself certain inexactitudes. For example, the Soho Waiters' Race does not immediately precede the Soho Ball.

The setting is obviously real, as are most of the streets, although some are not. Most of the locations are made up; real ones appear only when they have an innocuous role to play. Most of the characters are fictitious and bear the usual non-resemblance to any person living – I will not necessarily add to any person dead. Where real personages appear they have only walk-on parts.

K.W.

Author's Note

Since this is a work of fiction, I have permitted myself certain inaccuracies. For example, the Soho Women's Race does not immediately precede the Soho Half.

The setting is obviously real, as are most of the streets, although some are not. Most of the locations are made up, real ones appear only when they have an innocuous role to play. Most of the characters are fictitious and bear the usual non-resemblance to any person living — I will not necessarily add to any person dead. Where real persons appear, they have only walk-on parts.

K.W.

Prelude

Except for the City itself, which after working hours is left to the caretakers and the cats and the odd penthouse millionaire, there is no London neighbourhood more resembling the restless downstream tide of the Thames than the ragged square mile of Soho.

Ask Christine. Christine Yardley is literally here today and gone tomorrow.

Here is here and now, but by this hour her five-inch heels are teetering on the threshold of a new day. It is dawn turning to watery sunlight as Christine latchkeys herself through a narrow doorway next to the darkened lobby of a marooned bed show, the last of its line in Soho, in Hog Court off Greek Street. The bank of illuminated doorbells is dimmed now, and all the other girls in the house are asleep. Not that Christine is of their number: she pays her own rent.

She kicks off her crippling shoes and climbs the four near-vertical flights to her room – roomette would be a better word – at the top of the house. She flops down on the unslept-in mattress on a wooden base that passes as a bed and throws back her pretty head to guzzle down the last dribble of Diet Coke from a sticky can on the cluttered bedside table doubling as a dressing-table. She lights a cigarette from a new packet of Benson and Hedges, a little present from an admirer.

She unzips her rubber dress from Zeitgeist in Peter

1

Street and wriggles out of it. She adjusts her magnifying shaving mirror and removes her heavy makeup with Boots' No. 7, must remember to buy another jar. She takes off her ear-rings, her false eyelashes, and her long blue nail extensions, and pops them in the compartmentalised British Airways foodtray, breakfast size, which is where she keeps her trinkets.

She peels off her stockings and underwear. Perching her cigarette on the ashtray stolen from the ladies' at Soho House she levers herself into a corner shower cabinet the size of an upright coffin. The trickle of water is near freezing but she is careful to sponge away all traces of her heavy body perfume. She dries herself off and sprays herself with Sport deodorant. She shaves.

She tosses her underwear in the sink to soak. She rolls up her stockings and suspender belt and drops them in a deep cardboard carton, her underwear drawer, in the curtained recess that serves as a wardrobe. From another cardboard box she retrieves St Michael underpants and socks and dons them, then takes a shirt from a wire coat-hanger. She hangs up the rubber dress and takes down a grey business suit.

Soon Christine Yardley is dressed again, but not as Christine Yardley. It is Christopher Yardley who descends the stairs and walks around the corner to the Bar Italia in Frith Street. After a frugal breakfast of a caffè latte and a roll, he strolls along Old Compton Street, across Cambridge Circus to Shaftesbury Avenue and then to Holborn and out of Soho.

It is quite a walk to Fenchurch Street where, a Sohoite no longer until this time next week, he toils on VAT returns and suchlike for a firm of accountants, but he has all the time in the world before he must be at his desk, and he needs this break to adjust from one body to the other. This evening he will go home to his divorced mum in Ruislip, who thinks he spends these weekly nights away working at the firm's south coast branch in Bournemouth.

Christopher has been shuttling between one life and another in this way for five years now, and so far as he knows no one in the legitimate Square Mile has ever twigged his secret, although there was a narrow shave near Ludgate Circus once when responding to stares he discovered he was still wearing lapis-lazuli drop ear-rings, bad lapse, that. In the illegitimate Square Mile, of course, everyone is perfectly aware that Christine is a Christopher and that Christopher is a Christine, but they neither know nor care what persona he assumes away from Soho.

Live and let live, that's Soho's motto, if a pretty sanctimonious one at times. In any case, when it comes to passing off, the illegitimate Square Mile can no more lay claim to being an authentic square mile than Christopher can claim to be an authentic Christine. Nearer half a square mile would be more like it, if you lop off its adjoining territories such as the other side of the Charing Cross Road and bits of Covent Garden and a few streets north of Oxford Street, which are Soho spiritually but not quite geographically.

Not that Soho itself really exists as a map reference. As its self-appointed historian Len Gates points out at length to any tourist he can manage to ensnare whenever he comes across them consulting a map, it is not a borough, merely a parish – the parish of St Anne's, although the parish church itself was bombed flat in the war and only its tower remains. A parish, and a voting ward – of Westminster City Council, which from time to time in its planning zeal has done its best to remove Soho from the face of the earth.

But if that ever happened – and Len, puffing at his pipe and shaking the dandruff out of his off-white locks, is still full of fears when he sees yet another baker's shop becoming yet another boutique, just as in the old days it would have become yet another porn shop – Soho would simply spring up somewhere else.

For Soho is fluid. Gerrard Street, where it all began (Len will show you where Dr Johnson and his cronies used to hang out) is now the High Street of Chinatown and but an outpost of Soho, another of those adjoining territories which like Baltic states are of the neighbourhood yet not quite of its nationality. Soho's own High Street is Old Compton Street, its loose boundaries Oxford Street to the north, Charing Cross Road to the east, Shaftesbury Avenue to the south and Regent Street to the west.

Within these invisible city walls, Soho's permanent tally of residents these days, the rents being what they are, amounts to probably no more than three thousand souls, most of them living over the shop or more likely over someone else's shop. The strength of a sizeable village, which is what some of its residents sentimentally claim it to be. It's a matter of opinion.

Stephan Dance, not his real name but the one he chooses to go by, and the owner of three of Soho's surviving porn video shops, calls Soho his village because he has his breakfast croissant and cappuccino at Patisserie Valerie in Old Compton Street and buys his charcuterie and cheese from Fratelli Camisa in Berwick Street and his coffee beans from Angelucci in Frith Street. But Stephan takes his groceries home to Monk Wood St Mary's in Bucks, where he has a substantial ranch-style home, and that really is a village, with approximately the same number of residents. The difference is that while both in Soho and Monk Wood St Mary's Stephan Dance knows where to borrow a cup of sugar, in Monk Wood St Mary's he would be hard put to find someone prepared, at a price, to torch one of his three establishments, the loss-leader, for the insurance. Or alternatively, to burn down the rival sex shop over in Frith Place, for the increased turnover.

And something else that doesn't happen in Monk Wood St Mary's is that daily, nightly, shift by shift, Soho's population is swelled twentyfold by immigrants from the suburbs flocking in to work, or if not to work, then to eat, or drink, or loiter. Kitchen staff, bar staff, waiters, casuals, cashiers, cleaners, office workers, shop assistants, film cutters, dress designers, agents, solicitors' clerks, civil servants, market traders, bookmakers, hairdressers, craftsmen, club hostesses, hustlers, hookers, pimps, pushers and mug punters. People with homes to go to, when Soho has finished with them or they have finished with Soho.

But not all Sohoites are there daily, or nightly, to answer to the roll-call. There are those who are of Soho but, owing to circumstances, not in it. They set up their own Soho colonies in Notting Hill or Highgate or the Fulham Road where, playing by Soho rules – the main one of which is that any visible cashflow is communal – and conducting themselves as Old Compton Street remittance men, they languish in exile until, their sins expunged, their enemies now with fresher grudges, their debts paid off or more likely written off, they are free to edge back to the Old Country. There are pubs ten miles away from Dean Street that are spiritually as Soho as the French House. And doubtless there is a wing of Soho in Wormwood Scrubs.

This breed cross-hatches with another – those who are in Soho but not of it. We could find a good number of this type in and around Wardour Street, where the likes of Ellis Hugo Bell, a.k.a. Bell Famous Productions Ltd, have their offices and cutting rooms, many of them even smaller than the others.

Bell rather despises Soho, actually. Spent force. While he lives and works in a fourth-floor walk-up in Crispin's Yard off Wardour Street, where he rents a chamber the size of a restaurant cloakroom lobby which is his home, his office, and more importantly, his W1 postal address, he dreams of an apartment in New York City and another in Beverly Hills.

This will be when he has got his screenplay *Kill Me Nicely*, working title, off the ground. *Kill Me*, as it is colloquially known, at least to Bell, is based on an unpublished novel by a former flatmate, Kim Grizzard, a fact of which the author is as yet unaware since to acquaint him with the news would possibly involve Bell in paying for an option on the film rights, which he is not only unwilling but unable to do until he has got his deal together.

In any case, having changed not only the title but the storyline and the sex of the protagonist, he is in with a sporting chance of Kim never recognising it as his own work, especially if he is on one of his drinking jags when the movie is released. Kim's novel has a masochistic gay Soho waiter, a resting actor really, wanting to be strangled for fun and succeeding in this ambition. Bell has a masochistic cocktail waitress trying unsuccessfully to get herself murdered for kicks, being saved by the bell when her hired would-be killer falls in love with her.

6

He sees Madonna in the part, or maybe she is too old by now. All right, then he is thinking Demi Moore, he is thinking Sharon Stone, he is thinking Brooke Shields, he is thinking Linda Evangelista, he is thinking that stunning chick in the drinking-chocolate commercial, what's her name again?, if she isn't star material then Bell is no judge. To play opposite her he is thinking Leonardo DiCaprio, he is thinking Tom Cruise. At this moment in time it is all up in the air. Anything could happen. If he could get Daniel Auteuil then he would transfer the action to Paris. Take an apartment there. Rewrite the screenplay there. Or rather, write the screenplay there, since it has yet to be developed from a three-page outline.

And then – tomorrow the world. The penthouse. The platinum credit cards. The Porsches, plural. The membership of the kind of clubs that give you a gold key.

But first Ellis Hugo Bell of Bell Famous Productions Ltd has got to raise the sum of four hundred pounds, before he is once again welcome to cross the threshold of the Choosers Club in Greek Street, where you don't need a gold key or any kind of key but where your bar bill has to be paid up to date, and so does your dealer's. Bell owes a bar bill of nearly two hundred pounds, and the same amount, in exact figures, to his dealer, Danny.

Cashflow-wise, Bell Famous Productions has been going through a bad patch. There have been times when even though its chairman, managing director and principal shareholder has got the requisite gear, on credit, he has not been able to lay his hands on the equally essential ten-pound note to roll up for snorting purposes. Not that he really needs to snort, until he is seriously working on the screenplay, but to operate as a producer-writer-director (maybe not director: he is thinking one or two guys whose

7

names he cannot currently remember, but who appreciated the pitched outline) he needs to hang out with the kind of guys he needs to hang out with, and where are they to be found except in the Choosers? The Groucho? Soho House? No way. Wankers all – Bell has been there.

But the Choosers has begun to shake its head at him, and Danny, at the end of the bar, if that's where he is, or downstairs in the marble-flanked washroom if he happens to be doing business at the moment, has taken to holding up two fingers. Bell Famous Productions is – only temporarily, of course – in hiccup mode. Two fingers means two hundred and it has to be found twice over, before he can even begin to dream.

Unsentimental Ellis Hugo Bell, who is not strong on research, either into his own mercurial projects or the mercurial mini-planet he finds himself inhabiting, wouldn't properly realise that even beyond the chrome and glass confines of the Choosers Club (known to *Private Eye,* inevitably, as the Losers Club), he walks in a realm of dreamers. Had he ever allowed Len Gates to grasp his sharp lapel, he would have known that it has been so ever since Soho was invented, with the ultimate purpose of accommodating, in the fullness of time, the likes of Bell Famous Productions Ltd.

We have to go back in time, and then fast-forward. Seen through a camera's viewfinder, Soho (as it would not occur to the pedestrian Len Gates, to whom history is buildings, to look at it), has known three periods – sepia, black and white, and colour. For anything earlier you would have to look in a print gallery, at those so-elegant, so Len Gates engravings of grandees in their grand town houses in grand squares, before the refugees came teeming in from every ghetto in Europe, with their

8

shoemakers' lasts and tailors' thimbles and lacemaking machines and carpenters' tools and watchmakers' lenses and jewellers' scales, to transform the parish of St Anne's into the seething mini-cosmopolis it has ever since been.

In its sepia days Soho was a honeycomb of one-room workshops, delicatessens, charcuteries, coffee blenders, newsagents, cheese importers, wine shops, barber shops, shoemakers, jewellers, pubs, tobacconists, open-fronted greengrocers whose pyramids of oranges spilled down into the gutters, and dozens, no, scores, of cramped little cafés and restaurants, French, Italian, Greek and German. Old Jakie, selling his *Evening Standards* at the side of the Prince Edward Theatre, a pitch he has known since it was the old London Casino, remembers eating three courses for one and thruppence in those sepia days, when the riot of bleached shop blinds gave the corner of Old Compton Street and Dean Street the look of a three-masted schooner in full sail.

There is a touch of the sepia about Old Jakie himself. Nobody knows quite how old he is but he goes so far back that when he was born over the Welsh Dairy in Romilly Street it wasn't yet called Romilly Street, but Church Street. Old Jakie's first job on leaving Soho Parish School in Great Windmill Street was delivering milk to the cafés and tavernas from that same Welsh Dairy. Then he sold papers, as he does now. Then he was a market porter in Berwick Street, scene-shifter at the Apollo Theatre, window-cleaner, bookie's runner, three-card-trick frontman (the ostentatious 'winner' who pulls in the punters), amusement-arcade minder – and all without setting foot outside Soho. Then the Welsh Dairy was turned into a sex shop and he worked there for a spell too – back to square one, as he used to say.

Old Jakie is so ancient, and so sepia, he can remember your so-called Bohemians trickling across into Soho from what they used to call Fitzrovia, after the Fitzroy Tavern – North Soho or NoHo as some of them call it now, or NoGo as irreverent Soho has it. Artists, poets, that crowd. That Augustus John. That Dylan Thomas, piss artist he was supposed to have been. But Old Jakie had never seen him handle more than a half, and that he made last all night. The French pub he used to use, they all did. And there was one reason and one reason only why they deserted Fitzrovia and took up Soho in Old Jakie's opinion, and that was because south of Oxford Street the pubs in those days stayed open half an hour later. And that was why they came, for that last half-hour. And when the pubs closed they either went on to the old Gargoyle Club or the Café Royal, where so long as you had a sandwich in front of you, you could drink till all hours. Old Jakie knew that for a certain fact because he had worked in the Café Royal kitchens, washer-up, ten bob for the night, and come closing time the waiters would barge in through the green baize door with these plates of sandwiches the punters had left, because all they wanted was the drink; and that would be Old Jakie's supper.

There were many other things Old Jakie could remember, including how long since he had been barred from the Coach and Horses for doing so at length. These days he reminisces only briefly, and by request. This is seldom forthcoming, for considering its colourful past Soho is surprisingly unnostalgic – it has always lived for the day.

Black and white Soho comes next in the album – its best days, according to some. The war years and beyond, when the whole neighbourhood was seen through a pall of cigarette smoke (it has since become a 'City of Westminster Air Quality Improvement Area'), and the girls, or Fifis as they were known, were as thick on the pavements as the pigeons in Trafalgar Square. All street life was there. Archer Street seethed with out-of-work musicians hanging around outside their union offices, hoping for session jobs. The shop doorways, where they didn't harbour hookers, accommodated chefs and their commis coming up for a breath of coffee-scented air. Skulking dirty macs in search of what Soho calls 'the Vice' contrasted with expensive camelhair overcoats draped across Italian shoulders. Clusters of drinkers, like witnesses to an accident, would congregate outside the French House – still, then, called the York Minster – and the Coach and Horses. Everyone wore a hat, and everyone was smoking.

Somewhere in that black and white montage you should find Else – Else for Elsie? Else for Elspeth? No one has ever known her first name, let alone her second – probably lighting one of her customary panatellas from the gasolier on the mahogany counter of the old cigar store on Old Compton Street. It's a boutique now. As is Old Jakie's Welsh Dairy, which first became a sex shop.

Soho wasn't Soho without Else. And, even more alarmingly, still isn't. She is one of the fixtures, a kind of human bollard.

She was a pretty young thing in those black and white days, Else. She always claims to have modelled for Francis Bacon and maybe she did, though nobody has ever seen the end result – it would probably look nothing like her, by the time he'd finished – which she says is owned by a rich New York collector. Augustus John she sat for: that's well known. There are sketches and photographs of Else by lesser lights, when she was young and beautiful. Trouble is, she's barred from most of the places that have them on their walls.

Even back in that black and white era, you couldn't take Else anywhere. But then you didn't have to – she *was* everywhere. If you went into the Coach, she was in the Coach. If you left the Coach and went into the French, she was in the French. These days, of course, you won't find her in either place, or in any other pub that has seen her coming. That's because over the years Else has got into the unfortunate habit of incontinence. So if she has managed to get into one or other pub while the guvnor's back was turned, you can always tell she's been by the faint whiff of panatella smoke, the faint whiff of Else, and the little damp patch on the bar stool where a cat with kidney trouble might have been dozing.

But that's now, with Soho in living colour, when the likes of Else are not wanted. Then was then. In the black and white days Else was the life and soul of the party. A fixture in Aux Caves de France, but if you got fed up of buying her drinks – she was rarely in a position to buy drinks herself: no money, honey – and took yourself off to the Colony Room Club two doors away, she would have got there before you. The Colony Room, still known as Muriel's although it's years now since Muriel went under the sod. The Gargoyle. The Kismet, a.k.a. the Iron Lung. Why did they have all those clubs – over four hundred of them in and around the district at the height – when Soho itself was one big club?

We move on. The old Iron Lung is now a pizza parlour. The butcher's in Brewer Street has become a champagne and oyster bar. Ten years ago it would have become a sex shop. Nowadays in Soho it is easier to buy a Filofax than a filthy mag, and easier to get a vodka martini than have your clock repaired, and the girls sipping their house bubbly in Kettner's Champagne Bar who call themselves models, really are models this time round, limbering up for the Soho Fashion Fair at the Café Royal. We are in colour.

Most of Old Jakie's distantly remembered Bohemians are long gone, dead of cirrhosis of the liver or retired to the country or gone legit with Arts Council grants and BBC contracts. Ellis Hugo Bell, thinking Courtney Love, thinking Minnie Driver, is, along with his Wardour Street friends and enemies, a more typical Soho habitué these days; and the state-of-the-art chrome and glass restaurants and open-fronted cafés, with their tiled floors and bent-wood tables, more typical than the nicotine-drenched wining and dining garrets of Soho's black and white and sepia periods.

As Old Jakie tells it, a local authority which once actively encouraged the bulldozing of Soho, to replace it with thirty-storey bleeding tower blocks, a six-lane bleeding highway and elevated bleeding concrete walk-ways from Oxford Street to Shaftesbury Avenue, finally decided that if it couldn't beat them it would join them, and after initially resisting the spread of pavement cafés on the grounds that they would impede any two handi-capped people trying to pass one another in wheelchairs (only Jeffrey Bernard was passing by in a wheelchair, and he didn't mind), it eagerly did its best, as is the way of city councils after the reprieve of a disastrous planning decision, to back-pedal by gentrifying the area to within an inch of its life, with hanging flower baskets, cobbled pedestrian areas, and a sanitised street market. Len Gates approves: he calls it regeneration. Old Jakie has another view: 'If they can't fuck it up in one way, they'll fuck it up in another.'

But you can't keep old Soho down. Behind the designer glitz and the chrome and the black leather armchairs there still survives more than a goodly handful of sex shops and strip shows – ask Stephan Dance, although he'll say the game is finished; and models of the old sort still occupy second-floor walk-ups in the newly cobbled alleys, although more discreetly nowadays, behind their lit-up doorbells. And there are still a few of the old Soho drinking clubs. The Colony Room is still there. Gerry's Club is there, and thriving. So is Kemble's, the rival actors' club, and struggling. The old Kismet Club in Great Newport Street is, as we know, no more, but the new Kismet Club at the end of Frith Place, no relation, staggers on.

According to Mabel, who owns the place, there won't be any drinking clubs like the New Kismet still going a year or two from now, not the way the licensing laws are being liberalised. There aren't all that many of them left now – a dozen, perhaps, if you're talking about ordinary drinking clubs, places you'd once go to when the pubs had to close in the afternoons, as against gambling clubs, most of them in Chinatown, or clubs for specialised trades such as waiters or chefs or criminals.

Golden days, Mabel calls that wonderfully repressive era when you couldn't get a drink legally for fourteen and a half hours out of the twenty-four. Her membership register was like a starstruck fan's autograph book – Charlie Chaplin, Bing Crosby, Humphrey Bogart, Laurence Olivier. And then there were even those who came off the street and signed themselves in under their own names, for some strange reason. Genuine addresses too, in some cases. You'd think they wanted to be arrested.

Mabel had opened the New Kismet when the old Kismet in Great Newport Street had closed, and she had never looked back until just lately. Afternoons only the New Kismet was these days, three till seven, that was enough for Mabel at her age, then they could bugger off back to the French or the Coach or wherever they wanted. It is getting so it is all the same to Mabel whether they come down or not. Time to be putting her feet up. Little place in Brighton. Soho by the Sea.

'Are you a member, sir? Go on, then, fuck off, this is a private club,' she calls mechanically as young James Flood tentatively rounds the bend in the shabby staircase. Mabel models herself on the legendary Muriel Belcher, of the Colony Room Club, for whom she did the odd stint as a barmaid back in the old black and white days. The cattier members say she has borrowed Muriel's pugnaciousness but none of her personality.

Too late James Flood recalls that he really is a member – one of a tiny select band who have actually paid over their twenty-five pounds dues and received a grubby pasteboard oblong in return. Too late Mabel remembers it also – he has bolted.

Poor James is too young and too nervous to be working in Fleet Street – certainly too young and too green to be on the Soho beat. The Soho beat is a new venture for the daily *London Examiner*. Its editor Jane Rich, herself newish, was dining in the Groucho Club one evening when the celebrated television personality Brendan Barton was escorted out for urinating into a plantpot. It occurred to her that there must be a

15

thousand news stories in Soho. There are indeed, but none of them has as yet been divulged to young James, who has been assigned to the task of finding them. Soho knows how to keep its secrets.

Certainly there would have been nothing for him in the New Kismet where the only other customer, at this hour, getting on for seven, is Jenny Wise, actress, nursing her last triple brandy, no ice, no soda. If young Flood watched more old films on the box he might just have recognised her. He would half know the name, anyway. In her day Jenny Wise was going to be another Julie Christie, but then she didn't quite become it. She did get some star billing back in the mid-sixties, though. Big mates with Diana Dors, Bonar Colleano, that crowd, she was. Invites to all the openings at the Odeon, Leicester Square. No stranger to the White Elephant, where Rex Harrison once blew her a kiss.

Jenny, now, is a bit of a link between the Soho of Old Jakie and the Soho of Bell Famous Productions Ltd. Old Jakie, from his flyman days, remembers her playing the juve lead in some play or other at the Apollo – always very nice to him, she was, gave him many a fag. Ellis Hugo Bell, for all that he is definitely not thinking Jenny Wise – he is thinking Kate Winslet, he is thinking some of these new models, that's if they can act – knows her from *Halliwell's Filmgoer's Companion* and the Sky Movie channels. That *Tell Me Tomorrow* was her big break, playing opposite James Mason. Then a couple of others, more downmarket, more B-feature, you were then thinking Eric Portman, you were thinking that fellow who finished up doing voiceovers. And then nothing. The usual route. Arms like a dartboard by the time she'd finished, silly bitch – not that Hugo hadn't tried shooting up, but he didn't have to be at Shepperton at six the next morning, did he? – and then when she'd got herself weaned off that, the booze. The hard stuff. Still not yet sixty, still keeping her looks although she's getting fleshy with it, she has her regular stool at the end of the bar in the New Kismet, the one always occupied in Soho clubs by ladies of a certain age who seem to celebrate a lot of birthdays.

Worked on, there could be a story after all in Jenny Wise for the Soho correspondent of the *Examiner*, if only she wasn't speechless. By this time of the evening, Jenny can only slur.

'Come on, Jen, let's have you pissed off up them stairs to Bedfordshire,' says Mabel, not unkindly. As always, she asks: 'Now are you going to be all right?'

Yes, Jenny will be all right as she pushes her brandy aside for tomorrow, gathers up her bits and pieces and gropes her way up the stairs, with Mabel behind her to put the chain on the door and catch her if she falls. She's only to get across to her little flat in Charing Cross Road where she will crash down until three in the morning, breakfast time.

As Jenny's day ends, so Soho's begins. Ronnie Scott's will be tuning up by now, and the Raymond Revuebar throwing open its doors. Give the drag haunt Madame Jo-Jo's, a favourite with Christine a.k.a. Christopher, a couple of hours yet, but most of the club bars and pubs have already filled up. Soon the greeters will be taking up their posts in the smart new brasseries, and the waiters will hover anxiously in the doorways of the dingy old restaurants as if fearing they will never see a customer again. There is not a table to be had in the pavement cafés, the human flotsam and jetsam are crowding the streets now, the traffic is crawling, the discreet illuminated doorbells glow as dusk closes in.

It is another day beginning in Soho, one day like any other day – that is to say, different from every other one.

I

Butterfield's Rhubarb Farms Ltd, of South Higginshaw, just outside Leeds, had a firm policy guideline for its truckers: no hitch-hikers.

This was because one of its lorries, in the old pre-refrigeration days, had been hijacked at air-pistol point and made to drive across the Pennines to Rochdale, where the gunman's auntie, from whom he had expectations, was terminally poorly. By the time thirty tons of rhubarb finally made it down south it had gone limp and the wholesaler was not best pleased.

But Dave Boothroyd, driving an articulated eighteen-wheeler down to New Covent Garden, liked a bit of company, what with the terrible reception he was getting on Radio 5 Live, the only station he ever listened to. Even in this high-tech age the tachograph didn't show if you stopped to give some poor bugger a lift, and another thing: there was an old Spanish custom that the hitcher stood you a fry-up at the Happy Eater south of Doncaster.

'Don't see you in the Miners much these days, kidder,' said Dave over two rashers, egg, sausage, beans, black pudding and fried slice. The Miners Arms, South Higginshaw. Changed its name to the Cross-eyed Beagle after a makeover, but was still, to its regulars, the Miners.

'No, I been spending moster my time in Leeds,' said Alex Singer. Alexander to his mum, Alex to his muckers,

Al to close friends, Ali to the girl-friend. 'Did do, before she pissed off.'

'You're at the uni, aren't you, Alex?'

'Metro, yeh.' Leeds Metropolitan University, third year, media studies.

'I might be wrong, kidder, but didn't you have a bit of a beard, last time I saw you? Little goatee?'

'Chin beard, yeh yeh yeh.'

'Excuse me, Alex, but I was under the distinct impression that the biggest majority of beards grew on chins. As I say, I could be wrong.'

'It's what they're called, Dave – chin beards. They're like a style statement.'

'So what happened to it?'

'Shaved it off, didn't I? She didn't like it. In fact she blurry hated it.'

'Why – tickled her muff when you went down on her, did it?'

Alex thought this a touch offensive, coming from someone he barely knew, in fact had never spoken a word to until he'd thumbed a lift on the South Higginshaw slip road. On the other hand, he had to get to London. Urgent. Top priority. Alex said nothing.

Dave mopped up egg yolk and tomato pips with a morsel of fried bread. 'So what's she called, this lasser yours?'

'Selby.'

'Selby!' echoed Dave scornfully. 'That's not a fookin lass's name, it's a fookin town.'

Privately, Alex took the same derisive view. And indeed, it was not her proper name. She had changed it, against his advice, from Sheilagh. It was one of the things they'd rowed about.

'So is she at the uni as well, this Selby?'

'Metro. No, she's a nurse, Leeds Infirmary. Off to be, anyway – trainee. Was. Before she walked out.'

'And why do you say she gave you the Spanish fiddle?'

'Come again?'

'Spanish fiddle. El bow. That's what your Cockneys call it. The Big E. The elbow.'

Good one, that. El bow. He'd remember it.

'I didn't say why, Dave, but if you must know, it was the culmination of a lotter things. She says we're not compatible. Could be right.'

Could be at that. She wanted to live down south – came from it, near enough, Peterborough – where he didn't.

'And what makes you so sure she's buggered off to London, Alex? Is that where she said she was off to?'

'Didn't tell me nothing, Dave. Just said she had to think things out, switched off her mobile and pissed off into the night, like I said. No, it's just my intuition sorter thing. If she was going anywhere, and she was because she's taken most of her gear according to her mate, she'll have gone to London.'

'She coulder gone to Peterborough, if you say that's where she comes from. Gone home to Mum.'

'She came up to Leeds to get away from blurry Peterborough, didn't she? Couldn't stand the dump. No, I'm telling you, Dave, she's in London, and I've a good idea where.'

'So have I, kidder. I don't want to worry nobody, but King's Cross, that's where she'll have landed up.'

'Not Selby, mate,' said Alex, with the quiet smug confidence of the twenty-one-year-old in love.

'I'm telling you.'

21

'You don't know her, Dave, never met her. She's not that type.'

'Once they're over the river Trent, kid, they're all that type. I'm not out of order, I'm saying nowt against the lass, it's just that once they're down there, they get sucked in. It's crawling with pimps and ponces is London, they get sucked in. Can't help themselves.'

'Not my Selby.' Alex knew all about King's Cross. Had never been there, never been south of the river Trent himself, matter of fact. Donny – Doncaster – that they'd just by-passed, that was as far south as Alex had ever been, or wanted to go. By road, that was. Muster passed over whatever all them places south of Donny were, Newark, Retford, time he flew Leeds-Bradford to Barcelona with a buncher mates for the World Cup game, and what shite that turned out to be. Then there was that weekend in Jersey with Selby, coupon offer in the *Yorkshire Evening Post,* first time they'd ever had it away together. Christ on crutches, was she up for it or was she up for it? If only he could get her in Jersey now, tonight, tripette down Memory Lane, it would be all sorted, no probs.

But the only time Alex had set foot in Donny itself was when he and a crowder the lads from the Metro had rented a mini-bus and come down clubbing one Friday night. Coupler them had heard that this venue called the Glue Works, other side of Donny getting on for Newark, was where it was all going on. Going on up Alex's arse, it was crap.

'Ever heard of a dive called the Glue Works, somewhere round here?' he asked Dave. They were back on the road.

For a casual question, designed to get Dave off his insistence that Selby could only be working the streets of King's Cross, it evoked a curiously cautious answer.

'I mighter done, why?'

'Just went there one time with summer the lads, that's all. Didn't reckon it. Is it a drag joint, Dave? Because if it isn't, there's a lorrer talent round Donny haven't half gotter five o'clock shadder problem.'

'I wouldn't know, Alex. When I'm on the road I'm on the road, most exotic place I ever see is the Happy Eater where we just was.'

At least this pointless exchange had had its desired effect. Or so Alex was hoping, in vain as it turned out. As they passed a grassed-over slag heap with the window-less shed that was the Glue Works, a former working-men's club, perched on the side of it, Dave added: 'Not that I've ever been in it since it was the old Colliers' Institute, but if as you say it's turned into a drag joint, you're not gunner find her in there, are you?'

'I never said I would, Dave. She's not left Leeds juster finish up outside Donny. No, I know where she'll be all right.'

'So do I, lad. Take it from me, King's Cross.'

'Can we drop it about maring King's Cross?'

'So where else might she have headed for, you tell me?'

'No might about it, Dave. I'm telling you, I know. So-oh.'

'So-oh? What would she be doing in fookin So-oh? There's nowt there for a lass on the run in this day and age, kidder. It's all changed, has So-oh. They've cleaned it up. It's all caffies and coffee bars these days, hardly any red light district to speak of at all. So you'd be wasting your time there.'

'How many more times, Dave? She's not a maring hooker, she's a maring nurse. Be told!'

'There's a lorrer lasses nowadays is both, Alex, lad.

Nurse by day, streetwalker by night. Or t'other way round if they're on night shift. It's not their fault, poor kids, they just don't get paid enough. And besides, the punters like the uniform, they go mad for it. So I've been told,' added Dave virtuously.

Alex, deciding that Dave was either insensitive or incorrigible or both, or perhaps plain dim, again tried to get off on a different tack.

'When will you be going back up to Higginshaw, Dave?'

'Tomorrer dinner, soon as I'm loaded up with some seedless grapes for Leeds Market. Why, you don't want a lift back, do you?'

'Wouldn't mind, if it's no trouble.'

'You've not even got there yet. You're never gunner find this lasser yours in twenty-four hours, you know.'

'I've got to, Dave, otherwise she's had it. I've gorrer job interview day after tomorrer.'

'Oh aye, who with?'

'I'm saying job interview, it's with what they call a head hunter. Sorting out applicants for jobs on Radio Metropole.'

'Never heard of it.'

'You won't've done, Dave, it's not started up yet. Only they're recruiting nearly everybody from scratch, so I'm in with a better chance than I would be with the Beeb or Radio Aire, where they won't even look at you if you've got no experience.'

'Experience at what, kidder?'

'DJ. I'd be good at it, I know I would. I've done a coupler discos at the Metro Union, standing in forrer mater mine, and from what everybody says it seems I've got what it takes.'

'And what does this Selby reckon to it?'

'Norrer lot, Dave. She thinks I'm reaching for the moon styler thing. But as I've said to her, a lorrer people've reached for the moon, and summer them have got to run with it.'

Another subject for a row, could have been, but he'd refused to rise to it. 'Anyway, we'll see. All I want is a foot in the door and then it's up to me, innit?'

'Nonner my business, Alex,' said Dave. 'But are you sure, deep down, you really want to find this lasser yours? I mean to say, from all you've said, you don't exactly seem to see eye to eye.'

They were bypassing Peterborough. Sod Peterborough.

'I know it sounds like that but as I say, Dave, you don't know her,' said Alex doggedly. But he took Dave's point, he had to admit it.

What he didn't tell Dave, and what he hadn't told Selby, was that this head hunter story had got a bit out of hand. True, a bloke from Radio Metropole was coming to talk to the media studies course, but no way could he be described as a head hunter, he was just marking their card on job prospects in radio and that. But Selby, for the sake of picking a row, had chosen to believe he was a head hunter, and Alex, for the sake of preventing a row, had gone along with it, to the point at which he now more or less believed it himself.

Another thing he hadn't told Dave was that he wouldn't be so much looking for Selby in Soho, although he would certainly be on the look-out for her. No: with any luck, she would be looking for him.

He had told that lass Selby shared a flat with, Vicky, that he was going down to London for twenty-four hours, all the time he could spare, and would be searching for Selby in Soho, where she was likeliest to be. Vicky was in touch with Selby although she denied it, lying little mare that she was, and would pass the message on. If Selby wanted to be found, in the few short streets that comprised Soho from what he had gathered, it should be the easiest thing in the world to make herself visible. If not, sod her. It was make or break time. Put up or shut up.

He was putting Selby to the test, that was the size of it. She'd said she was leaving Leeds 'to think things out'. Well, he'd given her nearly a fortnight to do it in, hadn't tried to persuade her not to go, hadn't come running after her, but now this was it. The crunch. The Radio Metropole bloke might not be exactly a head hunter but he was a valuable contact and Alex wasn't going to let the opportunity slip past him by hanging around in fookin London. If she hadn't thought things out by now she never would.

Of course, he had no proof positive she had headed for London, but if she'd pissed off to Dublin or somewhere, Vicky would have given him the wink. It was Vicky, in fact, who had tipped him the wink about Soho. The pair of them had done a weekend in London before Selby became an item with Alex, and they were forever banging on about this So-oh place and how some prat had taken them into this flash club called the Groucho and poured champagne down their throats. He'd like to get the full story of that one of these days, but he didn't suppose he ever would. Besotted by So-oh, though, Selby was. Knocked out by it.

'So what you gunner do when you've found her, kidder?'

'Play it by ear, Dave. I meaner say, I'm not gunner drag her back up to Leeds by her hair, am I?'

'Just so long as you face up to the chance she might not want to see you.'

No way, if she didn't want to see him all she had to do was go to ground for twenty-four hours. Stay indoors.

'We'll have to see, Dave, won't we?'

'I mean, if as you say she's not answering her mobile, it doesn't bode all that well, now does it?'

No. And he hoped to Christ she was answering her mobile to Vicky, that they'd fixed up some kind of code between them, otherwise he was in it without a paddle.

Dave's tea-time. They pulled in at Scratchwood Services to take on sausage rolls and doughnuts. Christ, he could shift his food, could Dave. The way this trip was working out, it would've been cheaper to take the fookin coach.

The first snag was that Soho wasn't on the tube, as Alex was to discover upon Dave insisting on depositing him at King's Cross with the words: 'She might be working the street here, kidder, or she might not, who am I to say, but if it just turns out she is and you've done nowt about finding her, you'd never forgive yersen, now would you?'

It seemed convoluted logic to Alex, but unlike the airgun hijacker he could not order Dave to take him where he wanted to go, so he climbed out at the main line station.

Piccadilly Circus was on the tube map but not Soho. Paddington, St Paul's, Hyde Park Corner, hearder them, but where was So-oh? It wasn't on the bus map either. To the best of his recollection it wasn't even on the Monopoly board.

So where was it, then? Alex realised belatedly that he had not the slightest idea. He had never asked Selby, didn't give a toss where it was, got bored by her talking about the place. Subject of another row, that was.

Limehouse seemed to ring a bell, so did Chelsea. They were the kind of places you read about in the same breath as Soho, but they weren't on the tube either. Limehouse was on a line that didn't seem part of the Underground system, called the Docklands Light Railway, starting from somewhere called Bank, but that looked blurry miles away. Come to think of it, Soho was more likely to be up West somewhere, round about Piccadilly Circus, that way. Selby had said as much, insofar as he could recall.

Should've asked Dave when he had the chance. But Dave would only have said: 'Bugger So-oh, I'm telling you, she'll be in King's Cross.'

He consulted an Underground inspector, who told him to take the Piccadilly line and get out at Leicester Square, stupid pillock that he was. Alex took the Piccadilly line and found it had already been to Leicester Square and was now decanting him at somewhere he'd never heard of called Caledonian Road.

The warm May sun was setting over the London Hippodrome by the time Alex finally emerged from Leicester Square Underground. A news-vendor told him, apparently as a matter of policy, that he didn't give directions, but a kindly American tourist who'd heard him ask the way to Soho guided him along Charing Cross Road and told him to make a left at Shaftesbury and a right at Greek, Frith or Dean till he came to Old Compton.

Neither Greek nor Frith looked promising, they were just ordinary streets. What looked like Chinatown was across the road, at least the street signs were in Chinese and the telephone boxes were got up to look like, what were they called, pagodas. Were there a lot of Chinese in Soho? Could be that the Yank meant him to take a left rather than a right at Greek, Frith or Dean. He couldn't be sure – maybe it was Limehouse, he'd read in an old Sherlock Holmes story that it was teeming with Chinese and opium dens. But he remembered from the tube map: Limehouse was somewhere else.

He pressed on to Dean Street. A bank, a McDonald's and one of that chain of takeaway sandwich joints that were springing up everywhere. He wouldn't mind betting there'd be a fookin Starbucks round the corner. Christ, he could've got all this in Leeds without moving away from the Headrow. If this was So-oh, Alex didn't reckon it. Couldn't work out what she'd seen in it.

But maybe it wasn't Soho. He'd bought a map at the King's Cross tube station bookstall but that had no mention of Soho in any shape or form whatsoever. Soddin place didn't seem to exist. As he pored over his map, trying to place Leicester Square as a starting point and succeeding only in finding Westminster Bridge, an Essex voice behind him – Alex recognised estuary English, gorrer lot of it at the Metro – murmured: 'Nice club you're looking for, young man? Nice bed show, only one in town. Show's just beginning and you're obliged to buy one drink only, two if you want one of the girls for company, and I promise you'll come out with your wallet intact, it's cheaper down there than Titanic, I'm telling you.'

Alex didn't even know *Titanic* was still on or what it had to do with it but he knew a club tout when he saw one, they had a couple in Leeds, up Chapeltown, red light district. Bloke who looked as if he doubled as the bouncer, black suit, knuckleduster rings, standing in a narrow doorway leading to a steep, darkly lit staircase that could have you going arse over tip if you'd had a few, which you would've had to have had to fall for that liner patter. Yeh yeh yeh, this was So-oh all right.

'Tell you what I'll do with you, young man. Two for one – buy one drink, get a second one free.'

Ta but no ta. Alex knew all about these places from the Sunday tabloids. They got you down there, fetched you a glasser piss, hostess comes over, orders champagne, gets a bottler piss-coloured water and the next thing you know you've got a bill for two hundred quid and the bouncer is frogmarching you off to the nearest cashpoint.

'Just looking, mate,' he said and moved on. The tout called after him: 'Well, go fackin look somewhere else, northern git.'

Charming. He reached the corner of Old Compton Street. Shoe shop. Pub. Wine bar, looked like. Alex still wasn't totally convinced he was in Soho. He approached an elderly man who was hovering on the corner. Pipe smoker. Thick glasses, mane of dirty white hair, tightly belted raincoat. Weirdo. Looked a likely customer for that bed show clip joint down the street.

''Scuse me, mate, which is So-oh?'

'Soho, my friend,' began Len Gates in his high, braying voice, responding as though Alex had pressed a button and switched him on, 'is less a location than a state of mind.'

Oh, Christ, place milling with people and he had to go pick on a fookin nutter.

'Now I myself am in Soho, and perhaps you are in Soho. But that man over there,' Len nodded towards an overalled workman striding purposefully along the other side of the street, 'is not in Soho. To him, this is merely the conduit to Cambridge Circus, there to the east.'

Complete and total dork. 'So is this So-oh or not?'

Ignoring the question, Len Gates evangelically took Alex's elbow and began to steer him, as if to Mecca, along Old Compton Street. 'Yet unbeknownst to our friend, Old Compton Street, besides comprising the very heart of Soho – for yes indeed, you are in Soho, young sir – is one of the most fascinating thoroughfares in London. Originally Compton Street, it was named after one Henry Compton, Bishop of London, founder of St Anne's which is our parish church, and Dean of the Royal Chapel, hence Dean Street which we have just left. Now I imagine you watch television. Number twenty-two Frith Street here was where John Logie Baird—'

'Some other time, mate, just seen a bloke,' gabbled Alex and, like some aircraft passenger being hustled down the emergency chute, hurled himself through the swing doors of the pub they were passing, leaving the startled Len Gates standing on the corner of Frith Street to await his next victim.

Jumping Jesus, they knew how to charge for lager down in London, didn't they? They muster seen Alex coming. Tasted like catpiss, too. But it was all he was going to get, because Christ alone knew what they were charging for shorts.

Money was going to be a problem, even though he was only down here for twenty-four hours. He'd drawn exactly fifty pounds, all but cleaning out the account, and already he was breaking into his second ten-pound note. Two fry-ups, two goes at the sausage rolls and doughnuts, map, two tube tickets, pint, it was melting away like blurry snow. He would just have to ration his spending through the night and tomorrow morning. Where to sleep? Park bench, he'd think about that one later. Thank Christ he'd arranged with Dave to give him a lift back, because if he didn't find Selby he would've otherwise been in shtuck.

Selby would have readies, she always did. Enough to stand her round, anyway, and more than her round when Alex was skint. Nice little flat she shared with Vicky. Holidays she could afford – that trip to Jersey, even though it was a bargain offer, she'd more or less paid for it. Alex sometimes wondered where she got it from – not from the fookin hospital, that was for sure, the wages they paid. She was supposed to have come into a little nest-egg from some uncle of hers, but Alex had never been completely convinced about that, she'd always been a bit evasive on the subject.

'Not Selby, mate, she's not that type,' he'd said to Dave, but you never knew, did you? He wouldn't admit it to himself, but when Dave dropped him off at King's Cross he'd had a good look around before going down into the Underground.

And what was this fascination with Soho? From what he'd seen of it so far, there was more life in piggin Manchester if she'd wanted to take off somewhere. It wasn't Dave who had planted doubts in his mind, truth to tell, they were there already.

What he should've done was to go down into that bed show club, show them the photo he'd got with him, see if any of them knew her. But he'd been afraid to go down, hadn't he, because he'd be scalped for certain sure.

Having brooded into his lager for long enough, Alex took stock of the pub he was in, the Princess of Teck. Cramped little place, dark wood, old photographs of boxers, needed a makeover. Taking in the customers, he had to admit that, dweeb though he was, the saddo who had grabbed hold of him on the corner back there did have a point. Some of these characters were definitely Soho, you could tell that a mile off, while some were, how should he put it, obviously just passing through, kinder punters you'd find in any boozer from here to wherever. But some of them, most of them in fact, looked like regulars, and what they had in common apart from them all being blokes – were there no women in Soho? – was that they didn't look to Alex as if they held down jobs. Oh yes, yeh yeh yeh, they might do some kinder work for a living but no way did they do anything whatsoever for most of the day except go on the piss, you could tell. He knew now for a certain fact that he was in So-oh.

The podgy type standing at the bar next to him, sipping what looked like a large G and T, or it could've been just designer water he supposed, although from the fleshy jowls and broken veins that seemed unlikely, nodded at him in what Alex took to be a sophisticated metropolitan manner. Self-consciously he nodded stiffly back. He had never exchanged nods before.

'So what brings you to the Great Wen?'

Great when? What the fook was he talking about? Were they all bonkers down here or what?

Familiar face, couldn't place it, though. Fruity voice. Actor, could he be?

'Come again?'

'What brings you to London?'

Alex found the assumption that he was a tourist, a bog-trotter, mildly patronising.

'How do you know I don't live here already?'

His interlocutor looked benign. 'Accent you could cut with a pair of garden shears, haircut by some High Street plonker calling himself Mister Scissors, suit that looks as if it came from the Fifty Shilling Tailors, *circa* 1963, need I say more? One doesn't have to be Sherlock Holmes. But I didn't know they were still making suits like that. You'll have picked it up at the Oxfam shop, I imagine.'

Alex, his head swimming rather, decided on balance not to take offence. It was just the guy's manner. Also, he was half pissed.

'It was my dad's, if you want to know. I got left it.' It was only the third time he'd ever worn the suit, or any form of suit – once at his dad's funeral, once at his Metro interview, and now. He'd decided on the suit rather than his usual gear in case he had to go into any of these clubs like the Garrick's where you had to wear a tie.

'I don't particularly want to know, if you want to know. What are you doing dahn t' Sarth?'

'If that's supposed to be a Yorkshire accent, you need to work on it.'

'Nevertheless.'

'If you wanner know—' he had to stop saying that, it sounded defensive '—I'm looking for a lass. A girl.'

'Then you've come to the wrong shop. You'll have noticed, none of us are lasses here.'

Yeh yeh yeh, he had noticed all right, but he hadn't got the Princess of Teck down as a gay pub, they all looked too butch for that, including this beefy bugger. Alex knew a gay pub when he saw one, they had them in Leeds. The Ironmaster in Vicar Lane for one, known as the Aintree Ironmaster.

He had definitely seen this bloke before, knew him from somewhere. He put the thought into words. 'Don't I know you from somewhere?'

'I should bloody well hope so, otherwise my living has been in vain.'

Alex had got the bugger now. It was him, wasn't it? Whatwerehecalled? Him on that programme.

'It's you, isn't it?' he said, as many had said before him.

'It is me, or should I say it is I? Grammar was never my strong point.'

It was already too late to ask this famous bloke, and he certainly was famous, for his name. Alex would have to go back to the Metro Union bar and say: 'Tell you who I had a long chat with down there, bloke who used to do that programme Sunday nights, *Books and Persons*. Norrer bad bloke, bought me a drink.'

Brendan Barton was in the act of signalling the bar staff for just that. He reached out a podgy hand bedecked with heavy rings like the knuckleduster jewellery of the chucker-out at the bed show club.

'And your name is . . .?'

'Alex. Don't have to ask you yours' – although he did.

'You'd be forgiven if you did, since I haven't been on air for the last nine months.' Oh, Christ, yeh yeh yeh, Alex had gorrim now. The stupid sod had done an interview with some famous writer or other completely rat-arsed, and they hadn't renewed his contract. What was his soddin name?

'So what did you make of the programme, such as it was?' asked Brendan Barton.

'I only ever watched it coupler times, but tell you the honest truth, I thought it was shite.' Alex believed, erroneously, that as a Yorkshireman he was expected to be blunt. He didn't really think the programme was shite, he had no opinion about it one way or the other.

But the TV personality did not seem in any way offended. Inscrutably, and purring to himself, he said: 'I'm sorry not to have pleased you. I can see that I must be penalised for that.'

Was the bugger being sarky, or what? But Alex was not to be enlightened, for at this point a diversion was created by the entry of Old Jakie the news-vendor from across the street, or rather of the late Old Jakie's limp body, carried in by two of the flymen from the Prince Edward Theatre.

'Where shall we put him, Ronnie?' called one of them.

Emerging from a back room, the bad-tempered-looking landlord did a double-take at the sight of Old Jakie's body and uttered: 'Jesus Christ Almighty, is he dead?'

'Looks like it to me, Ronaldo,' said the other volunteer pallbearer.

'Sod me, what was wrong with him, was he ill?' asked a whisky drinker at the other side of Brendan Barton.

'Course he was fackin ill, he's fackin dead, isn't he?' snapped the landlord. To the flymen, who were holding Old Jakie like a sack of vegetables they had come to deliver to the kitchen: 'So what happened?'

'Just dishing out an *Evening Standard* to Michael here and he keeled over. Minds me, Michael, had you paid him?'

'No, course I hadn't, what was I supposed to do, put pennies over his eyes?'

'So what was his problem?' asked the landlord.

'You mean apart from being dead? Dicky heart, I'd say.'

'All right, and so why have you brought him in here? This is a pub, not a flaming morgue.'

'We thought it was what he would have wanted, Ronaldo. After all, he's been coming here for how long?'

'Too bloody long. Go on, then, sling him along the bar counter and I'll ring for an ambulance.'

As willing hands cleared ashtrays and glasses off the bar, and the two flymen respectfully laid out Old Jakie as in the undertaker's parlour where he should more properly have been put to rest, Alex, speaking from medical knowledge gleaned from Selby, piped up: 'They won't come.'

'Who won't come?' asked the landlord aggressively.

'The ambulance service. They won't take away dead bodies.'

'Oh yes, and how many dead bodies have you seen being left to rot in whatever pub you grace with your presence, which certainly isn't this one? Practising coroner, are we?'

'No, but I do know what I'm talking about.'

'You know sod all, son. This'll be the fifth stiff to leave these premises in my time, and they've all left by ambulance.'

'Mickey Ryan, dropped dead where I'm standing now,

37

Boris the Boxer, keeled over down in the bog, Nellie that used to pose for that what was his bloody name, John Minton, fell off her bar stool and never got up again, and who was the other one?' intoned a glum-looking Scotch-drinker who evidently regarded himself as the pub archivist.

'Complete stranger, knocked back three triple brandies, fell back on his head like a planker wood, never seen him before or since.'

'You certainly wouldn't have seen him since, Ronnie, unless you went to the funeral,' put in Brendan Barton.

'Which I didn't, and I shan't be going to this bugger's neither, money he owes me,' the landlord said.

'Bitter respect, Ron, he ain't even cold yet,' said the pub chronicler. 'And could be your oldest customer we're talking about.'

'Oldest customer here, Coach, French, anywhere between the Crown and Two Chairmen and the Pillars of Hercules,' said another.

'Makes one wish for a hat, so that one could doff it,' said Brendan Barton.

'How long *had* he been coming in, Ronaldo?' asked one of the flymen, acknowledging with a tip of his glass a complimentary half of bitter for services rendered.

'Christ knows. He was a fixture when I moved in, and we're talking 1963 now. Used to be in your liner work that time, scene-shifter, sunnink. As he never stopped telling us.' The landlord gazed with something approaching fondness at the body laid out on the bar. One of the flymen had folded Jakie's arms in the approved laying-out manner, so that without his cap he would have looked like one of the stone effigies in Leeds Parish Church graveyard, where Alex used to go snogging. 'Gor, you could bore for England, couldn't you, Jakie?'

'But you never barred him, Ronaldo, unlike some licensed premises we could name.'

'Couldn't afford to, he had too much on the slate. By Christ, though, he could knock it back, couldn't you, Jakoh?'

This was definitely one for the lads back at the Metro. Blurry pub turned into a blurry mortuary, stroll on, you wouldn't get this at the Miners Arms.

'Member time he had that ruck with who was it having a go at him that time, you barred him, Ron, didn't you?'

'Too bloody true, cheeky sod. Charlie Fish, works in Berwick Street market. Why he used to drink here insteader the King of Corsica bang next to his stall we shall never know.'

'He was barred from the King of Corsica,' the second flyman said.

'More than likely. Anyway, this time we're talking about, Jakie here had a bundler late *Standards* under his arm and he wouldn't let Charlie look at one to see what had won the last at Sandown. He goes, "If you want a free read, get down Westminster Public Library." So Charlie goes—'

'"You're the second biggest prat in Soho."'

'Go on, ruin the fackin tale. He goes, "Gawd, you're a prat, Jakie. Shall I tell you sunnink? You're the second biggest prat in Soho." So Jakie goes—'

'"If I'm such a prat, why ain't I the first biggest prat in Soho?"' recited the second flyman.

'"Cause you're a prat,"' supplied the first flyman.

'Am I telling this fackin story or are you two? So that's when Old Jakie put one on him, tried to, anyway, but Charlie grabs his wrist. "Leave it out, you silly old prat," he goes. I says, "Right, that's it, Charlie, you're barred." He goes, "What you barring me for? He's the one that's doing all the aggro." I says, "Winding the poor bastard up, you know he's too thick to know what you're doing. Go on, out," I says.'

Second biggest prat in Soho. Good one, that. He could use that, could Alex. 'Do you know what you are? You're the second biggest prat in Leeds Metro.'

'Poor old Jakie, everybody used to wind the poor bugger up. Didn't we, Jakie? Member when somebody bet him the next person through that door would be a one-legged Chinaman?'

'It was Charlie Fish again. And Jakie couldn't work out that he could see the bugger coming in, through that window there.'

Brendan Barton knocked back his gin, causing Alex to suppose ruefully that it was about to be his round now. He could be skint by closing time at this rate. But Barton took his elbow – they seemed to go in for a lot of elbow grabbing down here – and propelled him to the door, murmuring: 'I fear we're in for a long night's journey down Memory Lane, if we stay here.' With an all-embracing wave: ''Bye, chaps.'

'Cheers, Brendan.'

At the door, Barton blew a kiss to the body of Old Jakie lying along the bar counter as on a slab. 'Sweet dreams, Jakie.'

Out in Frith Street the human traffic had swelled. Dusk was coming up and the people sauntering or in some cases bustling to and fro, mostly young and half of them clutching mobile phones, seemed drawn to the semi-darkness cushioning the pools of white light from the bars and cafés as moths were supposed to be towards the candle. Out to get their wings singed, some of them looked to be.

Three drifters greeted Brendan Barton who responded affably, clearly used to being addressed by complete strangers as they seemed to be. Alex was quite flattered that the telly star seemed to have adopted him. Course, it had to be said that he was pissed.

'The night is too young for wining and dining, so where to now?' asked Brendan, as if he regarded himself as Alex's host. 'But don't suggest the French, because I'm barred.'

'What's the French, then – wunner these clubs you hear about?'

'No, but it might as well be.'

Alex was still trying to work out the West End club scene. They had a different idea of what a club was down here. True, they had clubbing clubs with a disco and that, same as in Leeds – they were already queuing for one, the Limelight on the corner of Shaftesbury Avenue, when he passed it a few minutes ago – and then there were these clip joints, bed shows or whatever, that he was so wary of. They had the odd strip club in Leeds but no bed shows, he didn't even know what a bed show was. But there were these other clubs that you heard about or read about. The Garrick's, that was one. And what was that club Selby and Vicky had got themselves taken to?

'Why do you ask, my friend? Do you fancy a club rather than a pub?' asked Brendan.

'Leave it to you. Isn't there a place called the Groucho?'

'There is indeed a place called the Groucho, but unfortunately I'm non persona grata there at the moment, for the mortal sin of pissing on a friend from a first floor window. Had I pissed on an enemy,' continued Brendan Barton, 'they might have been more lenient. But if you want to see something of what now passes for club life around here, why don't we go across to the Losers?'

Funny name for a club. Maybe it was a gaming club, though you would've thought the Winners a better name for it. Alex hoped not, he wasn't getting lured into playing fookin blackjack or roulette or any of these poncy gambling games to please anybody. But when Brendan led him up Frith Street and he saw the brass nameplate on the wall of what looked like an old house, Georgian or something, same as you got in Park Square in Leeds where all the solicitors hung out, it turned out to be called not the Losers but the Choosers. They all seemed to have nicknames, these clubs. The Groucho, Selby had told him, was known as the Grouch.

While Brendan signed him in at a desk manned by two what the *Sun* would've called stunnahs, and so would Alex if Selby hadn't been on his mind, he examined a revolving display of free picture postcards. Yeh yeh, you could get them in Leeds, but there were some here he didn't know, the majority in fact. Advert for Eurostar, punter snogging bird: 'What do you recommend?' Waiter: 'A cold shower.' Londonnet.com.clubline: 'Arsey bouncers, get to know them before you go.' That'd go down well in Leeds. He pocketed a few.

They passed through into what was like somebody's big drawing room, or so Alex would have said, not having much acquaintance with drawing rooms. Fireplace, bookshelves, sofas, easy chairs, antique-looking tables, oil paintings on the walls. They sure had spent some dosh on this place. The only thing that separated it from being someone's home was that every single person in the room, and there were about twenty of them, was, with the exception of the two snazzy-looking waitresses, yammering into a mobile phone, like half the punters out in the street. All right, so everyone you saw in Leeds had a mobile, Alex had one himself, but they didn't make a religion out of it. It was like being in a fookin call centre.

Nodding and waving to everyone in sight – they knew how to make an entrance, these telly folk, say that for them – Brendan sank heavily into a leather sofa and beckoned Alex to join him. On the sofa's twin at the other side of a butler's tray table sat one of the mobile jabberers. 'I'm talking Gwyneth Paltrow opposite Tom Hanks, Mel Gibson directing. Unless David Beckham can act, because the two of them, Posh and Becks, could be magic.' Must be a film producer. Christ, he only looked Alex's age. Could be a wannabe, of course. So could moster the others in the room, them and their Filofaxes, now that he had them sussed out. They didn't half fancy themselves.

'Haven't seen you for a while, Brendan, what can I get you?' asked the snazzier of the two waitresses. Actress, she could've been. Maybe she was one. Resting. They did a lotter this kinder job.

It was the kinder job Selby might've taken, waitressing. Kinder job where you can get taken on by the day, it would just suit her, the way she was placed just at pres. He would have to keep his eyes open.

Well, she wasn't working at the Choosers, Losers, whatever they wanted to call it, so that was one place he could strike off his list. But he would have to do the rounds of as many of these clubs as he could, because they were a likely bet. Blag his way in, if need be. He was a good blagger, was Alex. He had blagged his way into half the clubs in Leeds.

'Yes, I've been staying with a friend in Somerset,' Brendan was saying. 'Or at least he'd become a friend by the time I left. I still have the scars to prove it.'

'You should be more careful who you choose as your

friends, Brendan. You'll get yourself killed one of these days.'

'If only. Now this young man is harmless enough. What would you like, Alex? I'm minded to give my guts a chance and switch to white wine for a while.'

'Same for me, ta.' He couldn't be doing with any more of that catpiss he'd been supping and no way was he going on to shorts, the prices they charged down here.

'Thank you, Libby, we'll have two large glasses of your fifty pee Chardonnay.'

'Now you know perfectly well we don't have a fifty pee Chardonnay, Brendan.'

'Yes you do, you charge four pounds fifty a glass for it.' And Brendan roared at his own joke and slapped his thigh as the waitress, with a pitying sigh, mock-flounced off to the serving hatch.

Yes you do, you charge four fifty a glass for it. He should be writing these down. He could use that in the Union bar back home. Except the stupid prats would get the feedline wrong. 'Fifty pee?' they'd say. 'Good to tell how long it is since you last bought a drink.' Forget it.

Four fifty a maring glass, though. And it would be his round next. Nine quid, ten if you had to bung the waitress as you would have to do in this kinder place. Jesus.

Ellis Hugo Bell of Bell Famous Productions Ltd, opposite, was concluding what was obviously only one of an endless series of calls on his mobile: '. . . I'm half in bed with a guy in LA whose name I daren't even breathe, but if he offers me anywhere near a deal I'd go for it and make it a co-production, fact with his name I'd settle for associate . . .'

He went on, having paused to await a reply that was evidently not forthcoming: 'So whaddya think?'

Alex knew what he thought all right. The guy was a tosser of the first order, a right wankah. But it had nothing to do with him.

'We'll talk, then. *Ciao*.'

The waitress brought over two brimming goblets of white wine. Cut glass, they were. They needed to be, at that blurry price.

Bell, not pocketing but depositing his mobile on the coffee table for immediate future use, picked up and toyed with a long-empty glass.

'Don't buy me a bloody drink, then, will you?' sighed Bell as the waitress hovered.

'Ah, you noticed!' boomed Brendan genially. Bell half shook his head, half helplessly shrugged at the waitress, who departed.

With an up and down, can-he-be-trusted glance at Alex, Bell then asked: 'I don't suppose you happen to have a line about your person, Brendan?'

Brendan, obviously feigning ignorance, asked innocently: 'A line of what, dear friend? Washing? Or in what? A line in repartee? I never give my lines away, they're far too valuable. If you mean the bottom line, then of course given the right bottom I could be interested.'

'Piss off.'

None of this meant much to Alex. It was how they talked to one another in this So-oh place. It was their manner of speaking.

He knew what a line was, of course. They were supposed to snort it off fifty-pound notes in these kinder places. Fact, from what he'd heard, most of the money circulating round here had been up so many nostrils you could score a hit just by opening up your wallet and sniffing it. Mary Jane, that's what they called the stuff now, so Selby had told him. In Leeds it was known as Bolivian marching powder. Not that Alex had ever done drugs, apart from Es or disco biscuits as they were known, and the odd puff of wacky baccy. Couldn't afford it, not on what he had to live on.

'Listen, I wanna ask you something,' Ellis Hugo Bell of Bell Famous was now saying. 'You're into S and M and all that, right?'

'Who says I am?' asked Brendan Barton quickly.

'Well, let's say you take an interest in that sort of scene.'

'I take an interest in music but that doesn't make me a pianist.'

'All right, then tell me this, Brendan, let's say from your wide knowledge of the world. Is it conceivable that somebody could deliberately get themselves murdered for kicks?'

'It's not only conceivable, it has actually happened,' drawled Brendan evenly.

'Blurry hell, where?' put in Alex, incredulous. Was he taking the piss? You just couldn't tell with this bloke.

'Southern California, of course, where else? Woman advertises on her web chat room for someone to come round to her apartment and strangle her. Murderer obligingly does so. She was probably getting a buzz simply from placing the ad, but in the event she was taken at her word – throttled with one of her own stockings. Killer never found.'

'Bollox.' This was from a young man who had draped himself over the back of Brendan's sofa while he called up a number on his mobile.

Without turning round Brendan said: 'Tell me, do your bad manners come naturally or did you have to go on a special course?'

Write it down, Alex, write it down. He could get a

reputation as the Metro wit on what he was picking up down here.

'The killer was never found because he didn't exist,' the young man persisted. 'It's one of these urban myths, like the dead granny in the car boot.'

What fookin granny? They were a difficult lot to keep up with, these Londoners.

Still without turning his head, Brendan asked conversationally: 'Do you know that game where you have to rearrange a number of words to make a well-known phrase or saying? Off fuck.'

Yeh yeh yeh, Alex knew that one. So did the young man. 'Bollox,' he reiterated as, unabashed, he wandered off, braying into his mobile: 'No, not you, Justin, I was talking to the second biggest prat in Soho.' Evidently they went in for recycling their lines. Just like Leeds.

'So when's this murder supposed to have happened?' asked Bell.

'Couple of years ago. Didn't you read about it?'

'No,' said Bell thoughtfully. 'But I bet I know someone who did. Listen, got a proposition for you, Brendan. How would you like to write the screenplay? Name in lights, eh?'

'Name in very small print, you mean. Not my forte, old man. Besides, I prefer to see my name on big fat cheques.'

'You'll get your big fat cheque with lots of lovely noughts, soon as I've got it all packaged, trust me. No? You'll regret it when you see the queues winding round your local multiplex.'

'No doubt. My life is a raft of regrets, heading for the Niagara Falls of disappointment.'

The things he came out with. Alex noted with alarm that, taking a generous swig of his wine, Brendan had already nearly emptied his glass. Bang went another tenner – and he'd probably have to offer one to this producer prat, too.

Ellis Hugo Bell persisted: 'Or if you want your money to do the work for you, you could always invest in a hundred-pound unit in my Internet project. Have I told you about *Walk On By?*'

'Frequently.'

'What's that then?' Alex thought to ask, not because he was remotely interested but because he reasoned that so long as the bugger was talking it would keep him from drinking.

'*Walk On By?* Simple. I mount a rostrum camera in a doorway – could be here, could be the Groucho, could be Kettner's, could be anywhere – and all we do, we film everyone walking past over the course of a day, unedited. Cut. Print. The National Film Theatre will give their eye teeth for it. Never been done.'

'Bollox,' snarled Brendan. 'That bugger Charles Pathé did it in the year fucking dot. It was a boring idea then and it's a boring idea now, but at least he had the nous to knock it on the head after one reel. You want to go on for twenty-four bloody hours. Who the fuck's going to watch it?'

'Anyone who visits bellfamous dotcom,' said Bell, the light of fanaticism in his eyes. 'If they'll click in to see a cigarette smouldering in an ashtray, which they do, why not hundreds of people walking past a doorway? And talking of walking on by—' Here, to Alex's relief, Bell seamlessly put down his empty glass, seized his mobile and shot to his feet. Gabbling ''Scuse, man, dog,' which Alex rightly interpreted as having to see a man about a dog, he bounded out of the room just as an unkempt, green-corduroy-clad figure, looking like the kind of lecturer who taught English but only to screw everything in sight, shambled across to fill the space he had vacated. While clean-shaven, he looked somehow as if he had only recently shed a beard.

Kim Grizzard was without a glass, that was the first thing Alex noticed. Nonner the buggers joining other people's tables ever seemed to have glasses. In Leeds, pubs, clubs, anywhere, if you joined a mate, you brought a glass over with you, you didn't expect him to get one in for you.

Kim, however, did not seem to have a drink on his mind. Glowering at Brendan he demanded: 'All right, shitface, when are you going to review my last fucking novel?'

Brendan, unperturbed, said: 'I'm doing you a favour in not reviewing it. It's unmitigated crap.'

'Good quality crap, though, admit it.'

With a formal sweep of the hand, Brendan said: 'Kim, I should like you to meet my young friend Alex. Alex, this is Kim Grizzard, the failed novelist.'

Alex wondered why no one ever put one on the cheeky sod. Or maybe they did. On the other hand, he was a beefy bugger. Looked as if he could take care of himself.

Without in the least acknowledging the introduction, Kim Grizzard, a self-obsessed berk in Alex's view, as moster them seemed to be in here, plonked down a fat, much-annotated typescript and said, not without pride: 'This is the next one. If you don't review this I'll never speak to you again.'

'You go on making these promises, Kim, but you never keep them. Under what title is it to be remaindered?'

'*Freeze When You Say That*, it's called. Guy locks his wife in the deep freeze because she's frigid.'

'Ah. An allegory.'

'A thriller. She gets out and goes after him.'

'*The Ice Maiden Cometh*. But why are you dragging the manuscript about London? Can't you find a publisher?'

'I have publishers beating a path to my door, but having had the one by way of celebration, I left it too late to get copies run off at Kall-Kwik.'

'That's how you propose to distribute it, is it?'

'Copies for my agent, berk!'

'A bit hard on Waterstone's, is it not?' enquired Brendan blandly. 'To have another Kim Grizzard thrust at them before the last one has been pulped?'

'You do come out with them, don't you, Brendan? All been used before, but you still come out with them.'

Brendan Barton bowed acknowledgement at the jibe, and allowed Kim Grizzard to change the subject.

Looking around the room and sniffing ostentatiously, Grizzard asked: 'What happened to the rancid pong I detected when I came in? I didn't see Libby with the air freshener.'

'Taken itself down to the bog, I imagine.'

'Home of bad smells.'

'Probably hoping to find something snortworthy down there. Ever the optimist, our Ellis Hugo Bell.'

'He'll be lucky. What's he doing, or claiming to be doing?'

'Oh, setting up an Oscar winner, as always. He's looking for a screenwriter, if you're at all interested.'

Alex, shrewdly for him, judged that Kim Grizzard, who in his early thirties or so did not look particularly well nourished, was interested although feigning otherwise.

'Why, what kite is he flying this time?'

'Christ knows. Care for a drink?'

'Scotch, please. None of your small ones.'

Oh, Christ. Alex might just as well go down into the bog and flush all his money down the loo. Funny how one minute they could be sitting there insulting one another, kinder thing you'd be invited to step outside for at the Leeds Metro Union, and the next be demanding large drinks off one another. Or rather, more to the point, off Alex, since there was no way of dodging his round.

Rigidly raising an arm and keeping it raised until he attracted the waitress's attention, Brendan continued: 'From what I gathered, it's based on that case two or three years ago where a woman in somewhere near Los Angeles deliberately set out to get herself murdered.'

Kim Grizzard, who like just about everybody else in the room had been agitatedly jerking his right leg up and down as if working an invisible treadle sewing-machine, brought this compulsive activity to an abrupt halt.

'It's what do you say?'

'Or on some kind of treatment based on the case, since he didn't seem to have heard of the true-life story. But he did ask me if it was conceivable that somebody could deliberately get themselves murdered for kicks.'

'I'll fucking kill him,' said Kim Grizzard very quietly, as in a trance.

'Why, are you claiming copyright? Come to think of it, I suppose it is the kind of crappy idea you might have used in one of your novels, Kim.'

'Did you say he was downstairs?'

'One imagines so. Search parties have not been sent out.'

The waitress was hovering. Alex had idly picked up a bar tariff card from the butler's tray table. Club whisky, six quid a shot. Jesus wept.

'Libby, my young friend and I will partake of two further glasses of your fifty pee Chardonnay, but this gentleman has a murder to commit, so he begs to be excused.'

'I'll commit it when the thieving swine comes back up

here. A public execution, this is going to be. Double Scotch, Libby, no ice. In fact make that a triple Scotch.'

Hellfire. Alex had a sudden urge to go to the lavatory. He rose stiltedly and in clumsy imitation of Ellis Hugo Bell's exit said: 'Dog. Bog,' and departed.

Long before reaching the bottom of the stairs to the gents' he had worked out the price of the round. Triple club whisky, eighteen quid, two glasses Chardonnay nine pounds, no way dare he ask for change out of thirty quid. Of course, there was always the possibility that Brendan might pick up the tab, but why the hell should he, he wasn't a charitable institution, and anyway, he wasn't working these days, was he? Alex determined to have his pee and slink off, having cut his losses. Not that, thank Christ, he had run up any losses so far, but he was getting the feeling he could be at a pickpockets' convention.

He found Ellis Hugo Bell of Bell Famous skulking in the lavatories, peering out of one of the cubicles. 'Is that prat in the corduroy suit still here?'

'Yeh yeh, he's talking to your mate Brendan Barton, he reckons he's off to kill you for some strange reason,' offered Alex helpfully.

'He's insane.'

'I reckon you're all fookin insane,' observed Alex, zipping up. Time he wasn't here. Sod paying thirty quid for a rounder drinks, anyway they were all nutters. He dried his hands, went upstairs, and left the club, ignoring the saucer of change, and there half-way down Frith Street was Selby, turning briskly into the cross-street.

3

Or at least he was ninety per cent sure it was Selby. Same hair, same ankles, same arse end. All right, so she was wearing a green jacket sorter thing he'd never seen before, but it wouldn't be Selby if she'd spent ten minutes in London without getting out her Switch card.

She was cutting along at a rate of knots, as if she were meeting someone and was late for it, along this side street called Bateman Street, leading into Greek Street as it would turn out. Hurrying after her, but refraining from calling her name in case he alarmed her and she made a run for it, Alex found himself obstructed by a mob of Americans as they seemed to be, at the vortex of which was Len Gates, rigidly holding up a furled umbrella with a stiffly raised arm in the manner of Brendan Barton summoning a waitress.

'. . . Now the hostelry you see across Bateman Street, the Dog and Duck, goes back to 1734 when gentlemen could shoot snipe in Leicester Fields nearby. Even earlier, there was another public house of the same name back there in Dean Street . . .'

Oh, do get outer the fookin way, you great useless lumper shite. Sidestepping the crowd, Alex was just in time to see Selby, if it was Selby, darting across Greek Street and entering a pub. Respectable enough house it looked, but it would be unusual for Selby to enter a pub, especially unescorted, wine bars were more her line. So could be it wasn't Selby.

He thought at first he was back in what was the place called again, the Princess of Teck? No, couldn't be, it was bigger, and anyway they were in a different street. Furthermore, from the Day-Glo menu advertising all-day sunshine breakfasts – £3.75 for a bowl of onion rings, by the left, you could get them for half that price at the Limping Tortoise on Leeds Bridge – it seemed to be called the Sun in Splendour, so that was that. Yet there was Old Jakie where Alex had left him, laid out on the bar counter like lamb and salad, now with fifty-pee pieces over his eyes, and there were the two flymen, together with a huddle of cronies from the Princess of Teck.

They recognised Alex. 'It used to be old pennies one time,' said the first flyman, explaining the fifty-pee pieces.

'That's inflation for you,' sniggered a young man in an expensively cut grey check suit, who looked as if he were no stranger to the racecourse.

'Bitter respect, James, he was a regular here,' said the gloomy Scotch-drinker, who had earlier set himself up as the unofficial archivist of the Princess of Teck, and now seemed to be assuming a similar role at the Sun in Splendour. To Alex he explained: 'He was staring, see, and we thought we saw his eyes move. They do, you know.'

'I don't think so,' ventured Alex respectfully, with his knowledge of morbidity gleaned from Selby.

'No, not that they actually do, but that you think they do.' And to the two flymen: 'Like when Nellie went over off her bar stool. I could've sworn her eyes were still moving when we picked her up.'

'That's because she wasn't dead yet,' said the second flyman. 'She died in the ambulance, if you remember.'

'Otherwise they'd never have taken her,' said the first flyman. To Alex he said: 'You were right, young man, the

54

ambulance won't take dead bodies in this day and age. At the death – I'd better put that another way, hadn't I? – in the end the guvnor had to ring the mortuary to send round a plain van. But apparently they can't do nothing till tomorrow morning, because they knock off at six.'

It was all great stuff for the lads but one thing was puzzling Alex. 'But what's he doing in here?'

'We're taking him on a last pub crawl, aren't we?'

'What he would have wanted,' said the second flyman.

The young man addressed as James scribbled a note on the back of his chequebook. 'Great story. Can I get your second names, chaps?'

Blurry hell, must be a reporter. Alex, who had vague aspirations in that direction himself should he fail to make it as a disc jockey, looked at the young man with a new respect. Fresh-faced, he was, looked as if he hadn't started shaving yet, too pink by far to be taken seriously. Could be a disadvantage in a journalistic career. Or maybe he lulled them by looking all innocent, Alex wouldn't know. He had only ever once met a reporter before, bloke from the local freebie who'd come to cover the Metro's annual fun run with Ronnie the Rhino as guest starter, but hadn't really got to speak to him. Bit of a twat he'd seemed – this guy looked to have more go in him.

'What paper do you work for, mate?'

'Work?' scoffed the Scotch-drinking pub archivist. 'Propping up bars from morning till night – you don't call that work!'

Like a stage magician producing the ace of spades, the reporter flashed a visiting card out of his top pocket and pressed it into Alex's palm. James Flood, Soho correspondent, *London Examiner*. 'Anything you've got, if we can use it we pay.'

'Ta.' Christ, he wasn't half seeing life. Talk about the fast track.

A flash of green, as Selby – was it Selby? – came up from the ladies' and crossed the room, heading for the double doors opening into Greek Street. Holy Jesus, with all this hoo-hah over Old Jakie's corpse, Alex had clean forgotten about spotting Selby, or thinking he'd spotted Selby. Was that a good sign or a bad sign?

Either way he was out of the pub like a bat out of a cave, catching up with the figure in green – for it wasn't anything like Selby – back on the corner of Bateman Street.

As he grasped her elbow, Christine Yardley, a.k.a. Christopher Yardley, almost wearily wrenched herself free as if being grabbed was a daily occurrence. 'Yes, what do you want?'

Husky voice, too much makeup, bit tarty, skirt too tight, and fishnets was pushing it a bit, but fanciable enough if you fancied them like that. But she was not Selby.

'Sorry, luv, I thought you were somebody else.'

'Oh, but I am!' pouted Christine, congratulating herself on her own wit. She got a lot of this.

'Sorry. Man. Dog.' This was rapidly becoming Alex's saying of the week. With a really fatuous grin he shambled off across the street and back into the Sun in Splendour, simply to get himself out of her eyeline should she be still gazing after him in puzzlement or pity.

As if Alex had never stepped off the premises, James Flood of the *London Examiner* continued: 'Or if you've got any useful contacts you don't mind introducing, there's always a drink in it for both of you.'

The phrase 'there's a drink in it' was both foreign and

distasteful to James, but he had been told it was Soho argot. For himself, he had been brought up in Maidstone, Kent.

While appreciating these handsome offers Alex felt in all honesty obliged to say: 'Wrong shop, mate. I don't know a soul in London.'

'You seemed to know our Christine well enough.'

'Mistook her for someone else, chum.'

'Not the first time it's happened,' sniggered James, unknowingly echoing Christopher–Christine's own joke. It was lost on Alex.

The landlady, as she presumably was, swept through the bar, bearing two plates of lasagne, it looked like. 'Seventeen, eighteen!' she bawled, and over her shoulder to the two flymen as she plonked the non-steaming suppers down before a couple of Americans who were sipping coffee in an obedient manner at a nearby table: 'I've already told you, I want that gentleman off that bar and out of these premises. He's barred, as he well knew and you well know.'

'But he's dead, Winnie,' protested young Master Flood of the *London Examiner*. 'Even you can't turn out a corpse.'

'I turn them out by the dozen every closing time, darlin,' said the landlady. 'Take him down to the New Kismet if you've got to take him anywhere. The state Mabel should be in by now, she won't know whether he's dead or just dead drunk. Come on, then, I shan't tell you again.'

The two flymen had made the elementary mistake of leaving their half-pints on the bar at Old Jakie's lifeless elbow. Winnie, by way of making her point, scooped them up. With martyred sighs, the flymen prepared to carry the dead body out, one attending to his torso, the other to the lower limbs.

'Could you open them doors?' requested one of them of no one in particular.

As Alex held open the doors and the mini-funeral procession proceeded with due solemnity on its way, James Flood, again producing the chequebook he had been told it was more prudent to use as a notebook in Soho than a notebook itself, murmured to Alex: 'Great tale. Dead man banned from Soho pub.'

The sharp-eared Winnie, who seemed to conduct all her observations over her shoulder as she went about her duties, warned as she sailed back into whatever cubby-hole she had emerged from: 'You print a word of this, young man, and I'll have your legs chopped off at the knees.'

'Oh, come on, Winnie, give me a quote!' pleaded James to her retreating figure.

'That was it, Jamie boy.'

'That's telling you, kidder,' said Alex, with a smug grin. The young reporter's discomfiture made him feel genially superior, if for no other reason than that it was James Flood rather than himself at whom the landlady was directing her condescension. 'Kidder' was not one of his expressions: he'd picked it up, not that he hadn't heard it a million times before, from Dave the truck driver. It would put James in his place as a southern wankah.

'It's what I'm up against,' said James Flood, with an echo of the flymen's hard-done-by sighs. 'There's a thousand stories in this square mile but every time I try to break one they fall on me like a ton of shit.'

'A thousand stories in this square mile' seemed vaguely evocative to Alex. Some late-night, grainy black and white repeat of an old New York City somethingth precinct cop series, was he reminded of? Anyway: he felt sorry for the poor bugger.

'Why don't we go after them, see if they take Old Jakie to where you'll get a better reception?' he suggested.

'Oh, I know where they're taking him,' said James. 'The New Kismet, as Winnie suggested. But they'll never get him down the stairs.'

In this, the Soho correspondent of the *London Examiner* proved to be mistaken, for Old Jakie was already *in situ* when he and Alex arrived at the New Kismet. The bar being too small to accommodate him, he was laid out on the floor where, through lack of space, Alex and his new friend James were obliged to step over the body.

Apart from the two flymen, the club was empty, although a still-life tableau of a glass of gin, a half-smoked cigarette smouldering on an ashtray improvised from an instant coffee jar lid, and a crumpled copy of the *Sun* open at the racing pages indicated the presence of Mabel. The flush of a lavatory cistern and she emerged to waddle across and resume her perch at the end of the bar. Alex studied her with some awe. Mabel's used face was not so much lived-in as owner-occupied. Her skin hung in loose folds as if put out to air and needing pressing. James told him later that a cheeky young actress had once been barred for life for asking whether, if she continued to cane the whisky and Coke at her present rate, she would finish up looking like Mabel.

Mabel snapped, with a distasteful glance down at Old Jakie laid out on the floor: 'I don't want him in here in that state. Anyway, he's not a member, so he can fuck off.'

'The cheeky sod, he's always said he was a life member!' exclaimed the first flyman.

'Dead member now,' cracked James Flood. Good one, that. Alex would remember it.

Mabel fixed a baleful eye on James. 'I thought I'd barred you.'

Fookin hell, they seemed to spend all their time barring people. However did they manage to keep any of their customers? Not that this dive seemed to have many. Maybe she'd barred them all.

'You didn't bar me, Mabel, you told me to fuck off because you said I wasn't a member,' said James, producing his grubby membership card. 'In fact I'm probably the only person down here who actually is a member. What are you blokes having?'

'They're having fuck all, because we're just closing. So come on, you lot, you can all piss off.' With a jab of her foot at Old Jakie: 'And take him with you. Wherever he's been to get in that condition, you can get your next round there.'

'Oh, come along, Mabel,' protested James. 'It isn't like you to turn custom away.' In fact, from the little he knew of Mabel, he couldn't think of anyone in Soho more likely to turn custom away, but he had a need to impress Alex with his worldly ways, just as Alex had a need to impress James with his. They were much the same age.

Clutching her stomach and wincing, Mabel said, in what for her was a kindly manner: 'Another time, Jamie. Tell you the truth, I've not been feeling too clever today, and I've got a hospital appointment in Soho Square first thing in the morning, so I'm banking on an early night and sod the lot of you.'

'Hospital for Women would that be?' enquired James Flood impertinently, clearly to show off his Soho knowledge.

'Mind your own fucking business and I'll mind mine.'

Heavy footfalls on the stairs, as of someone wearing

diver's boots, prompted her to look up. As on cue, Mabel went behind the bar and retrieved the half-tumbler of brandy that was waiting to be reclaimed by its owner. 'What the fuck are you doing here? I thought you'd gone home to bed,' she demanded, as Jenny Wise half lurched, half fell down the stairs.

Jenny had rules, or anyway a pattern. She would retire home after what she would call a day's jollies, usually unaccompanied although not necessarily so, at six p.m. or thereabouts, or whenever Mabel chose to close, and sleep until three a.m. She would then rise, shower and proceed to Kemble's Club for what she would euphemistically call breakfast – several stiff brandies and sodas, Kemble's being the only establishment that would serve her at such an hour. After a gulp of black coffee she would return home, this time not usually unaccompanied, at towards dawn.

But Jenny did not always play by her own rules.

'Couldn't sleep,' she slurred as she groped her way to the bar. 'That Charing Cross Road gets worse every night, keeping people up. Going write council, niff council won't do anything, move back to Denham Village. Noisy buggers.'

Alex recognised her, or at least he recognised that she was somebody, or once had been. By the left, you didn't half come across some famous folk in London.

'So you've still got half a million stashed away then, Jenny?' chaffed James Flood, with a man-of-the-world wink at Alex.

'Half million, what talking about, half million?' queried Jenny irritably.

'Property prices round Denham way these days. From what one reads.'

'Don't be ridiclous. I had most loveliest thatched cottage Denham Village considered overpriced by lawyer eight thousand pounds.'

'Long time ago, Jenny.'

Jenny what was her blurry name? Film star, was. Up there with Diana Dors, Dinah Sheridan, that crowd. Saw her in that shite with James Mason, only a few weeks ago. While not going so far as to belong to the Metro Film Society, Alex liked to watch an old late-night movie over a can of lager, if there was one on telly. Jenny Wise, that's who it was. Another one for the lads: 'Do you know who else I bumped into? That Jenny Wise. Yeh yeh yeh, her. Totally rat-arsed, she was. Out of her tree. Still good-looking, though, in fact a right cracker, considering she must be drawing her old-age pension by now.'

A swig of brandy had had the paradoxical effect of sobering Jenny up somewhat. If she had registered the prone form of Old Jakie lying on the floor, it was only now that she acknowledged the fact.

'If you ever see me like that, Mabel,' said Jenny, wagging a finger, 'just pour my brandy down the sink and call me a mini-cab.'

'If Mabel ever sees you like that, mate,' said the first flyman, 'she'll be calling Golders Green crematorium.'

A double-take from Mabel worthy of Jenny in her acting days, and then she shrieked. 'Do you mean to stand there and tell me he's fucking dead? You stupid bastards, is this your idea of a fucking joke? If the Club and Vice come down with this silly sod lying there, they'll go bald. Get him off these premises now, and don't come back. You're barred, both of you.'

'See you tomorrow then, Mabel,' said the first flyman. Unabashed, the pair resumed their burden.

'Say goodbye, Jakie,' said the second flyman.

'Let's take him to the Three Greyhounds,' said the first flyman.

James Flood, too, rose and reached for his hat. When Alex got back to Leeds, he too might start wearing a hat. 'Are you coming or staying?' he asked Alex.

'I'll stay here for a bit, if that's all right,' said Alex, avoiding Mabel's eye. Then boldly to Jenny, as the two flymen and James struggled to get Old Jakie up the stairs: 'Can I buy you a drink, Miss Wise?'

Making a coarse guttural sound, the first flyman urged: 'Get in there, son!'

'No, you can't buy her a fucking drink, you're not a member and anyway we're closing as soon as she's finished that brandy.'

'But I'm a member, Mabel, so if I order a drink and this young man gives me the money, that's all nice and legal, now isn't it?'

'You've had enough, Jen.'

'So what are you having?' asked Alex.

'We mustn't make this a habit, darling, but I could murder a bottle of champagne,' said Jenny.

You stupid prat, Singer. No one to blame but yourself. Teach you to keep your gob shut in future. And he didn't even like the stuff.

Mabel, with an unusual alacrity probably motivated by a suspicion that the self-blaming stupid prat might change his mind, dived into the fridge and produced a bottle of Moët something or other it was, which she displayed to Alex like a *sommelier*.

'Very nice,' said Alex, not knowing what else to say.

'That'll be thirty pounds,' said Mabel. Christ on splintered crutches. He was going to be left with less than ten quid out of fifty and he'd only been in London a fookin hour, if that. Talk about see you coming. And even though Mabel hadn't drawn the cork out of the bottle yet it was too late to get out of it now. Not that he really wanted to. In with a chance there, Alex, lad. Even if she's old enough to be your granny.

Or was this fantasy? No, it was beginning to look as if it wasn't.

For Mabel had no intention of drawing the cork. Pushing the bottle towards Jenny even as she closed a veined fist over Alex's reluctantly proffered three ten-pound notes, Mabel said: 'You can't drink it here, though. I'm just about to lock up.'

And Jenny said: 'Oh, do leave off, Mabel. I can't take him back to Charing Cross Road before I even know his name, can I?'

'It's Alex,' said Alex promptly. Now why did he wish he'd said, 'It's Dave'?

'Have I ever shagged you, Alex?' God almighty. They didn't care what they came out with down here, did they?

Feeling himself blush – when had he last blushed? When he'd peed himself around age six, far as he could remember – Alex responded gauchely: 'Not that I know of.'

'Believe me, honey, if we had ever got down to it, you sure would have remembered.' She did that in the dodgy Yankee accent he could remember her using in some ropy feature with Stewart Granger, was it?

'I'm sure I would.' Ingratiatingly to Mabel: 'Will you join us, Mabel?' For the idea of going straight round to Jenny's place frankly terrified him. What if he couldn't get it up? Not that he'd ever had problems in that direction, not many, anyway, and only when he was pissed, but this was a woman who muster had half the fookin film stars in England in her time, if not all of them.

'So how come you know my name?' asked Jenny coyly as Mabel, tacitly accepting his offer, pushed the bottle of champagne towards him. Oh shite, he'd never opened wunner these in his life.

'Have you got a corkscrew?' he asked. Jenny didn't quite stifle a giggle. Mabel breathed up her nostrils and took charge of the bottle. Oh, so that was how you did it. He'd remember that, for when he treated Selby to her first bottle of champagne. No, second bottle – she'd had one offer that bastard who had picked up her and her mate Vicky and taken them into that Groucho Club.

'Isn't he sweet?' purred Jenny. He blushed again.

'How come I know your name?' he reiterated brightly, to change the subject. 'Seen you on the box, haven't I?'

'Oh, yes, what in?'

'That loader shite you were in with James Mason, for openers,' hazarded Alex.

'I was in a lot of shite with James Mason. But are you sure you're not mixing me up with Margaret Lockwood?'

Irony was not Alex's strong suit. 'No resemblance whatsoever, Jenny,' he said. 'For one thing, you don't have that black spot on your cheek. You know, like Indians or is it Pakis have?'

'It's called a beauty spot, darling. And Maggy Lockwood was very beautiful.'

'So were you. Still are,' said Alex, with a clumsiness verging on the oafish. But Jenny smiled, if a little wistfully.

Emboldened by Jenny's directness of manner, Alex felt encouraged to ask: 'If it's not a personal question, did you ever get to shag James Mason?'

'It is a personal question, and the answer is that never having written my memoirs I can't possibly remember.'

'Maybe you're in his memoirs,' said Alex gallantly.

'I am, since you ask.'

Rather cheekily, Alex said: 'You used to be dead famous one time, didn't you?'

'Less of the used to be,' said Mabel, pouring champagne. 'She still gets asked for her autograph.'

'Even if they do think I'm Patricia Roc,' said Jenny ruefully.

'Who's she?' asked Alex. His knowledge of old films was not comprehensive.

'Before your time, darling.' Tiring of her own past as a subject, Jenny turned to Mabel. 'So when do you say your check-up is, Mabel?'

'For the third time of telling this very day, Jen, it's first thing tomorrow morning. Now get these bubbles down you, then we can all fuck off home.'

'You finish it, Mabel, it doesn't sit well on all that brandy.' Cheeky cow. Thirty quid down the drain. She might be a has-been, but she hadn't lost her Lady Muck ways. Carried on as if ten-quid notes grew on trees.

He would have to get his hands on some dosh. What he would do, he would get his mum on the mobile and ask her to pay some money into his account, first thing. Yeh yeh yeh, but it wouldn't clear in time, would it, and even when he'd tried to get an extra lousy tenner out of the hole in the wall earlier, it had come up 'Insufficient Funds'. All right, so she could wire him some cash. How would she do that, then from a little squashed fly on the map like South Higginshaw? He had seen adverts for Western Union but how you went about wiring money he had not the first idea. Neither would his mum, that

was for sure. So maybe one of his mates at the Metro
had a mate living in London who would sub him a few
quid. Fat chance. Oh, Christ. And where, anyway, was
Selby?

'You don't want any more champers, do you, Alan?'

'Alex.' No, pour it down the fookin sink.

'Alec.' She sounded half pissed again. 'Do you like
Scotch? I think I've got half a bottle at home.'

It's to be hoped so, luv, because here's someone who
won't be buying half a bottle if you haven't.

'Better than this muck we're drinking, it gives me
indigestion.' He ought to be eating something, but what
they charged for food down here, Christ only knew. He
shudder got more olives and crisps down him back at
that Losers place.

'Come on, then, I'm only round the corner. Nighty
night, Mabel, fingers crossed, hope all goes well.'

'So do I. And don't you dare come back this side of
tomorrow afternoon.'

She took Alex's hand and led him to the stairs, or rather
suffered him to lead her. The hand that squeezed his was
soft. Probably she was only squeezing to lend herself
support as she stumbled upstairs, but there was no doubt
about it, she was definitely up for it. Fookin stroll on.
He'd only been in London five minutes and already he'd
scored. What a tale for the lads. 'You're not gunner believe
this, but do you know who I got my leg across with down
in London? Member that famous film star, Jenny Wise?
Yes, you do, she was in a lotter crap with James Mason
and all that lot . . .'

Hold on, though. What if it got back to Selby?
She would give him the big E, pronto, wouldn't she?
The Spanish fiddle, as Dave called it. Or would she? There

was a certain what was the word, cachet, in shagging the boy who shagged the bird who once shagged James Mason, as she presumably had. He would have to think about it.

As they stepped out into Frith Place he was appalled to see Jenny raise her arm for a taxi. How did one countermand the gesture? Despite his standing behind her shaking his head vigorously, a cab drew up immediately.

'I thought you only lived round the corner, Jenny.'

'Yes, darling, but these pavements have a habit of going very wobbly at this time of the evening.'

His last fiver gone, then. Only loose change left. If she threw up in the cab he was in dead shtuck, because if down here was anything like Leeds they charged you twenty quid for having to hose it down.

Jenny's flat was a third-floor walk-up in one of the old Peabody blocks. Like a fookin tip it was, dresses and grubby underwear strewn all over the shop, empty bottles, dirty glasses, overflowing ashtrays, wire coat-hangers, piles of tabloids on every chair, a half-eaten cheese sandwich. Alex could do with that sandwich. He furtively nibbled a corner of it while Jenny staggered into the tiny kitchen.

Old cracked photographs everywhere, like in that first pub he'd gone to. Only these weren't boxers, they were film stars. James Mason, Eric Portman, Bonar Colleano, some that Alex didn't recognise. Signed with love to Jenny, or Jen, or Jens, or Jen-Jen. 'Lots of messages, Trevor Howard.' They were tucked behind mirrors or into the bookshelves, some pinned to the wall. They looked as if they had been in frames at one time, silver frames they'd have been and she'd hocked them. Down on her luck.

Jenny returned with two freshly rinsed tumblers and a half-bottle of Johnnie Walker. 'If you want soda, darling, you'll have to pop down to Thresher's and get some.'

'I can live without soda,' said Alex decisively.

'Help yourself, then. Water in the tap.'

Sloshing a couple of inches of Scotch into her own glass, she progressed with an unsteady, crab-like gait into her bedroom, at the first attempt overshooting the doorway but then more or less locating it.

So what was he supposed to do now, then? Follow her in, or what? If not, why had she left the door open? If she turned out to have zonked off, would it count as rape? Was he supposed to wear a condom? The number of men who muster gone through her in her time it would be wise, but he hadn't got any. And, that haunting refrain, supposing he couldn't get it up? If he didn't stop wondering that he would end up fookin impotent. Don't think about it, Alex lad.

These reflections were cut short by the re-entry of Jenny, and his fears of impotence dramatically reversed by the circumstance that she was completely naked. Christ almighty. Good bod, too. Knockers like chapel hat pegs. Waist a lass of eighteen woulder been glad of. Get in there, Alex, as the flyman had advised.

'So is it cold in here or what?' asked Jenny, with what sounded like asperity.

'Other way round,' said Alex clumsily. 'Since you took your kit off the temperature muster gone up twenty degrees.'

'Celsius or Fahrenheit?' Now she sounded scornful. 'So why have you still got your own kit on?'

The impotence threat returned, in spades. 'Waiting for you, wasn't I?' mumbled Alex. Jesus God, she was a goer, this one.

But it was to be all right on the night. She led him into the bedroom and he could only say performed, acted, presented, portrayed, personified her role as he had never come across it done before. Not that he had come across it done all that much. It was like being in a porno film. Maybe, Alex thought in a flash of panic, he actually was in a porno film – a set-up, hidden camera somewhere. At any rate it was all so slick that you couldn't tell Alex she'd never sunk to the depths of porn films in her time, poor cow. Depths? Who said depths? Maybe she enjoyed it. Certainly seemed to.

There were things he'd been doing with Jenny, or that Jenny had been doing with him, that he wouldn't half mind doing with Selby. Careful, though. He could see it all coming. So where did you learn that little trick from? You never used to do anything on those lines before you had your little spree in Soho, looking for me or so you claimed. Hm. *Joy of Sex*, that would hafter be the explanation. Found a copy lying about in the digs, didn't he?

But it was a one-off, seemed to be. Any expectations Alex might have entertained that he had found a billet for the night were exploded within the half-hour, by Jenny yawning: 'Time to move on, big boy.'

He was rather hurt. Had he been given a low rating out of ten? What – four? 'You want me to go?'

'We're both going, sweetie-pie. I need a drink.'

'There's still some whisky.'

'I don't need whisky, I need brandy.'

Oh, Christ al-bleeding-mighty, all he needed. So what did he do now, then? Confess he was boracic? Or bounce a cheque? Depended where she dragged him off to, though, didn't it? We have arranged with the bank that they do not sell beer. In exchange, they have arranged with us that we do not cash cheques.

'So where d'you want to go, Judy?'

'Jenny.'

Yeh yeh yeh, he hadn't forgotten that. Just getting his own back for her calling him Alan all the time he was shagging her.

'There's a club called the Choosers, commonly known as the Losers.'

Feeling ever so sophisticated Alex said self-consciously: 'Yeh yeh, I was having a drink in there with Brendan earlier.'

'Not Brendan Barton?'

'Right. Paller mine.'

'Christ. Alec, from your performance tonight you're the last person I would have thought was one of them.'

Flattering, if back-handed. Better put her right. 'I'm not wunner them, no. I didn't know for sure he was wunner them, although I did have my suspicions.'

'I don't believe he is "wunner them" in the sense you mean,' said Jenny. 'It's just that he has his peculiarities. Charming fellow, though, when sober.'

But Brendan was not sober, as Alex was to discover. Before that, however, there was an embarrassing exchange in the lobby of the Losers. Embarrassing for Jenny, that was. For Alex, it came as something of a relief.

It would have to be the bouncing cheque, he had decided, nothing else for it. Trouble ahead. The Yorkshire Savings Bank had already shown him the red card, threatening to shut down the account if he got overdrawn again. Over-overdrawn, that was to say. His mum had guaranteed his loan with not a lot to guarantee it with, and there would be hell to pay at home. Then he would have to find another bank, and who the fook would take him on? All in the interests of pouring brandy down the throat of an ageing actress who, all right, she was a terrific shag but the fact was, been there, done that, got the lovebites, and anyway, he was supposed to be looking for fookin Selby.

'I'm ever so sorry, Miss Wise, do you think we could have a word?'

The hotsy receptionist at the Losers. She smile-shepherded Jenny discreetly to the other end of her long desk. Meanwhile, down the stairs, which a sign indicated led up to the Choosers First Choice Restaurant, came Kim Grizzard, still clutching the now even more dog-eared and wineglass-rimmed manuscript of *Freeze When You Say That*. He did not recognise Alex. Come to that, Alex did not recognise him, although he knew he'd seen him somewhere during the course of what was beginning to seem like a long day, even though it couldn't have been above two hours since Dave had dropped him off at King's Cross. Eat, Alex, eat.

What went on between Jenny and the receptionist, Alex couldn't overhear, but it was plain enough what it was all about. Another barring job, wasn't it? Christ, if this lot refereed soccer teams, they'd never get to the second half. Talk about the red card.

'Sorry, darling, I appear to be temporarily persona non go and fuck yourself. Something to do with throwing up in the bog last night. Where do they want me to throw up – the Fifth Choice Restaurant? Fuck 'em.'

'So do you want to go somewhere else?' Shouldn't ask questions like that, Alex. She was quite capable of saying the Ritz.

Jenny passed a hand over a sweating forehead. 'I don't

think so. Alan, I have an urge creeping up on me to creep back into my bed, so I think I'll just creep away.' Rat-arsed. But as Alex took her arm to propel her out of the club, she pulled away. 'No, darling, you stay here, I have to get some shut-eye,' she insisted to Alex's relief. And to the receptionist: 'Is it all right if this very famous young gentleman stays on and has a drink? I'll sign him in if you like.'

'You're with Mr Barton, aren't you, sir?' asked the receptionist.

'That's right.' Must be still here, then. Stroker luck, could be. Casher cheque, give him the lend of a few quid – he looked like the type who would, if he felt in the right mood.

'G'night, sweetie.' As Jenny spun herself through the revolving doors, so Kim Grizzard, as if choreographed for a duet, propelled himself towards the reception desk.

'Is that cunt Ellis Hugo Bell still here?'

'Could you watch your language, please, Mr Grizzard? No, he left some time ago, I was told. By the rooftop fire escape, for some strange reason.'

'If he comes back, would you tell him I'm going to strangle him?'

'I'll see that he gets the message.'

As Grizzard shambled out, Alex passed through into the drawing-room sort of lounge which now, with the exception of Brendan Barton, seemed entirely repopulated with young women in black suits or black dresses, all clutching their Filofaxes with their mobiles tinkling like ice-cream vans, and all giving off the impression that they had just been or were on their way off to somewhere exciting, such as wunner these book-launch parties you sometimes read about. Alex wondered what they were like, these bashes they all went to down here. He wouldn't mind gatecrashing one. Blag his way in.

Brendan Barton was sitting, or rather slumped, exactly where Alex had left him when sneaking off, although by now clutching a glass of gin rather than the white wine he'd switched to. He was snoring gently.

Alex sat down opposite him, hoping that no waitress would approach before Brendan woke up, which he did almost immediately. Focusing blurred eyes on Alex he said: 'That must've been the longest shit in the entire history of defecation. If you happened to time it, you should write to the *Guinness Book of Records*.'

'Yeh yeh yeh, I got talking,' lied Alex.

'Did you say talking or snorting?'

This was a way in for Alex: 'Talking, I can't afford to snort. Listen, Brendan, I know this is a bit of a cheek, but I don't suppose you could lend me a tenner so I can buy the next round of drinks?'

Brendan garumphed. 'In this establishment, my fine northern friend, a tenner wouldn't even buy you a round of salted peanuts.'

'So call it twenty,' said Alex recklessly.

'Further to which, this is a club. You're not allowed to buy drinks, you're a guest.' Raising a stiff arm, Brendan summoned his waitress. 'Give this gentleman a glass of your fifty pee Chardonnay.'

'Yes, Brendan, we've had that joke.'

'It bears repetition. And an equally large gin, no ice, no tonic.'

Alex doggedly ploughed on. 'I've started so I'll finish. The thing is, I set off down here with fifty quid, reckoning it should be enough for just an overnight stay. But you must have roaring inflation in London because, what with one thing and another, it's gone. Blown, Christ knows where.' He thought he wouldn't mention Jenny and the thirty quid's worth of champagne.

'My dear, fifty pounds would just about buy you supper for one at a half-decent restaurant, provided you skipped the pudding and stayed with the house wine. Don't you have a cheque card?'

Another lie: 'Didn't think I'd need it.'

Brendan pondered briefly. 'I'll tell you what we'll do. I carry very little money in readies about with me, certainly not in the amount you'll need. But' – he lowered his voice conspiratorially – 'I do keep a certain amount of spot cash back at my flat in case of burglars.'

This had Alex puzzled. Brendan explained.

'You see, if you give them a fistful of used twenties, they'll beat you up but then leave in an orderly manner. Otherwise they trash the flat and take your valuables.'

'Sounds like you lose either way,' said Alex.

'Depends how one looks at it,' said Brendan cryptically. 'Now what do you say? Finish our drinkie-poos and all round to my place. I'm only up the street.'

With the uneasy feeling that he might be wandering into something of a honeytrap here, yet nevertheless realising that with barely the price of a hamburger about his person he didn't have much option, Alex dealt with the glass of wine that had just been set before him. How many glasses had he had so far? If Brendan really did mean to make him solvent for the night, he really ought to start keeping count.

It was only a few doors up Frith Street to Brendan's flat. A touch up-market from Jenny's place – four-storey, black-painted brick, bristling with solicitors' brass plates – Georgian, would it be? It seemed to Alex that everything around here earlier than the fifties and sixties was fookin Georgian. Historic, anyway, for around the threshold clustered a semi-circle of respectful Japanese tourists, submitting themselves to the lecturing of Len Gates: '. . . Now Frith Street, ladies and gentlemen, was formerly Thrift Street, and in this residence the composer George Frederick Handel is believed to have taken lodgings while his oratorios were being performed farther along the street at the house then belonging to His Excellency the Venetian Ambassador. Wolfgang Amadeus Mozart was also no stranger to Frith Street, where at the age of nine he lodged at the home of a stay-maker and performed at Caldwell's Assembly Rooms in Dean Street, alas like much else no longer standing . . .'

Seamlessly, as Brendan and Alex crossed the street and threaded their way through the throng of Japanese, Len Gates continued: 'Coming to the present day, ladies and gentlemen, this is also the residence of Mr Brendan Barton, the well-known television personality. Doubtless you are familiar with his programme in Tokyo. Good evening, Mr Barton.'

A polite twittering from the Japs as Brendan put his Yale key in the lock. Several of the tourists bowed. Some took his photograph. Brendan addressed a few words to them in what was presumably Japanese, clever sod that he was. Another for the lads. Alex would be a walking scrapbook by the time he got back.

If the hall with its black and white chequered tile floor, antique console table surmounted by equally antique mirror supported by gold angels or cupids or whatever they were was anything to go by, Brendan must have forked out a few bob for this pad. Didn't own it all, obviously. A trellis-doored lift rattled them up to the fourth floor, where it opened directly into the hallway of Brendan's flat. Snazzy or what?

Piles of new books in the hall, some still in their Jiffy-bags. Two cases of wine. Unopened letters, bills they looked like. And a curious item – a long riding crop in the umbrella stand. Maybe he went horse-riding on Rotten Row or somewhere. They did in that class.

Brendan led the way into what you could only call the drawing room, although he chose to call it the sitting room. Christ, the cost of the floor-length drapes alone could've put Alex through the Metro, and as for the furniture – not one but two sofas the bugger owned, chandelier, old prints on the walls, gilt all over the shop, it was like Templefookinnewsam Museum up in Leeds. For himself, Alex would have settled for the drinks cabinet, Chinese black lacquered, which when opened proved to be refrigerated, and from which Brendan extracted a bottle of champagne. Lanson, this one was. Alex was becoming quite a connoisseur.

Brendan carefully poured two flute glasses, cut glass like the Losers Club's but a better cut with it, or Alex was no judge. 'Make yourself at home, I just have to make a couple of calls,' said Brendan, and left the room, taking his champagne glass with him but leaving the bottle. Pity Alex didn't go much on it.

He wandered about the room. Like Jenny, Brendan went in for photographs, but his were properly framed, and all of them of himself with this or that celebrity. Authors, mainly, or anyway celebs who'd written books, and unlike Jenny's photographic friends, mostly still living. Well, they would be – they would all have been on Brendan Barton's programme, back in the days when he had a programme. There were two awards for it on the mantelpiece, a bronze-looking mask and an engraved what looked like a goldfish bowl. Arts Programme of the Year – three years ago. History. So why did publishers still send him books, then, when he could no longer plug them on telly? Maybe they thought he'd make a comeback. Maybe they were just big mates. Maybe – oh, Jesus.

Brendan Barton had returned to the drawing room. He was wearing a silk ankle-length dressing gown, more of a robe really, Chinese like his lacquered cabinet, and carrying in one hand the now vicious-looking riding crop from the umbrella stand in the hall, and in the other a packet of Walker's Chocolate Chip Shortbread.

Experimentally swishing the riding crop as if he had never encountered it before, Brendan said conversationally: 'Usually I accept two dozen, but if you took the view that more would be appropriate, I'm entirely in your hands.'

Wunner them, eh. S & M. Yeh yeh yeh yeh yeh, they haddem in Leeds too. Vicar, there was, ended up in the *News of the Screws*. Used to make his wife tie him to the copper and thrash him with a garden cane, poor bastard had to emigrate to New Zealand after the divorce had brought it all out.

Play this cool and careful, sunshine. They could be dangerous, summer these buggers, what he'd heard. 'Sorry, Brendan, wrong wavelength. This is where I get off. Makes an excuse and leaves, as they say.'

Brendan looked both pained and astonished. 'So after all you don't feel the need for a hundred pounds?'

What? 'A hundred what?'

'Smackeroos. In readies. In your back sky-rocket as we say south of Watford.'

Yeh yeh yeh, Alex had watched *EastEnders*. Loader crap, but he'd watched it.

A hundred. A ton as he'd heard it called, also on *EastEnders*. He said cautiously: 'That could just make a difference.'

'I'm sure it could. It could even be a hundred and fifty, if the service was up to scratch, if you take my meaning.'

Handing the riding crop almost ceremoniously to Alex, he peeled off the Chinese silk robe. To Alex's distress he revealed himself as revoltingly naked with folds of sagging white flesh, and wearing laddered fishnet stockings and twisted suspenders.

Oh, Christ. But a hundred was a hundred. Hundred and fifty, could be, so he'd said. Just so long as what he'd asked for was all he wanted.

'But on your perambulations through Soho, my stern young friend, I don't want this little adventure to get about.'

'You and me both, mate,' said Alex with feeling. 'Come on, let's get it over with.'

As he led the way through the hallway into his bedroom, Brendan Barton was still clutching his packet of chocolate chip shortbread. The hideous possibility flashed through Alex's mind that he might be required to do something unspeakable with them.

Stopping in his tracks in the bedroom doorway, where an antique four-poster loomed with black silken cords dangling from each carved post, he asked: 'What's with the packeter biscuits, then?'

Brendan pouted. 'I like to nibble a chocky bicky while it's all happening. Call me kinky if you like.'

4

As Alex Singer emerged from the house where George Frederick Handel had once lodged and Brendan Barton now lived, the two flymen were proceeding up Frith Street carrying the late Old Jakie on a makeshift bier consisting of an old door from a demolished building which they had requisitioned from a builders' skip.

Recognising Alex, the first flyman said: 'We've just tried to get him down the Blue Note.' Yeh yeh, famous jazz joint, even Alex had heard of it.

'Not that he was a member, fact he'd no interest in jazz as such, but he used to go down there one in the morning and sell the *Sun* and *The Times* first editions,' said the second flyman.

'But when we tried to get him down he slid off of the door, didn't he? Very steep staircase that, very.'

'So now we thought we'd double back to Dean Street and try the Crown and Two Chairmen. He often had the one in there.'

'You've lost what's-his-name, young bloke from the *Examiner*, James,' said Alex.

'Gone down Silhouettes, hasn't he? Sunnink about a book launch, sunnink.'

Alex moved on along Frith Street. As he neared the Choosers Club he thought for a moment that there must have been a fire alarm, for a stream of young women dressed all in black, sunglasses clamped over their heads, clutching their Filofaxes and still gabbling into their mobiles, was scuttering out of the club and into a building across the street, arms folded and shoulders hunched against the evening chill. If the two flymen had still been here with Old Jakie they could have passed as a funeral procession.

At this distance one, no two, no three of them could at an outside guess be Selby. Not that she ever wore black but down here in London you never knew, it made people do funny things, did London, as he for one could testify.

It was a flash-looking restaurant they were flocking into, brightly lit under a hanging sign, like a pub sign, of a silhouetted Regency buck and a crinolined lady. Silhouettes, then. Alex had assumed it would be another club but this should make it easier to get in. Some of the young women were carrying invitation cards but fook that, he would blag his way through.

Beyond the glass doors he could see that the greeter, who in her smart black suit could have been one of the Choosers contingent, was engaged in an altercation with a grubby old woman smoking a panatella. Could've been a bag lady if she had any bags other than the ancient tapestry handbag, its handle broken, repaired, broken again, which she clutched under her arm. Could be a good time to gatecrash.

'I'm sorry, Else,' the greeter was saying, as the young women in black streamed past her and up the stairs to the party. None of them was Selby. 'I've strict instructions not to admit you.'

'Yes, but why, my dear, surely you can tell me why?'

'Policy.'

'But you don't understand, I'm more entitled to be here than any of you young people. I tell you I knew him. I sat for him. I've been told even there's a pastel drawing of me in the book.'

'I'm very sorry, Else.'

She didn't sound it. Alex, on the other hand, did feel sorry for the poor old cow. In her way she was a similar case to Jenny Wise. Has-been. Down on her luck. Educated voice. Seen better days.

'Is that cunt Ellis Hugo Bell in here? He is, isn't he?' The slurring – for he had had a few since last encountered – yet still unmistakable voice of Kim Grizzard, as he slapped the tattered manuscript of *Freeze When You Say That* down on the greeter's podium.

As the greeter darted forward to bar Grizzard's progress and to deal with him in much the same manner as the receptionist at the Choosers had dealt with him ('He's not expected so far as I know, sir, but if you'd like to leave a name . . .'), Alex swiftly seized his chance. Taking Else's elbow, avoiding eye contact with anyone who might cast suspicious glances, and mouthing inanities such as 'And tell me, missus, do you come here often?' he steered her up towards the top-floor restaurant. Done this before, hadn't he? Bag o' Nails Club in Leeds with Selby, when neither of them had been a member, one of the few clubs up there where you had to be. Always some trouble on the doors at the Bagger Nails. You waited your chance and sailed in. Doddle.

There was a second greeter at the top of the stairs, clutching a little stack of invitation cards.

'Could I see your invitation, sir?'

'Er – ah. In fact I'm with James Flood of the *Examiner*. Just been out to get some fags.' He'd worked this one in Leeds too. Never failed, unless the person you claimed to be with either wasn't there or had already gone.

82

'All right, but I'm afraid we can't allow this lady in.'

'It's OK, luv, she's with me.'

'Yes, but you see, you're Mr James Flood's guest. I'm afraid you can't take your own guest in, sir.'

Alex felt like saying: 'Is there anywhere in this fookin town that lets anyone in?' Instead, and before Else could start on her own spiel about knowing whoever it was the book had been written about, he said: 'Yeh yeh yeh, but don't worry, she just wants to use the toilet.' Possession nine tenths of the law, that was the strategy: once he'd got her in they'd have hell's own job getting her out again without disrupting the party.

'That'd make a change,' was the second greeter's murmured aside to the ceiling. With a false smile to Alex: 'I'm ever so sorry, sir, it's not me, it's policy. So if the lady could kindly—'

'All right, where's that cunt Ellis Hugo Bell?'

Saved by the Bell again, as you might say. He'd work that gag in when it came to telling the lads the full story.

Kim Grizzard had half bounded, half fallen up the stairs, closely pursued by a burly, dinner-jacketed managerial type who was probably no more than a jumped-up bouncer.

'Now come on, Mr Grizzard, none of us wants trouble.'

'Who doesn't want trouble? You speak for yourself.'

The distraction was enough for Alex. He propelled Else into the crowded, half-darkened restaurant, where they were soon swallowed up among the chattering mass of freeloaders, as Alex judged the majority of them to be. Well, they must be, if even he and Else had managed to get in, and that ace wankah Ellis Hugo Bell was here. James Flood would have got an invite of course, being press, but a lotter them, apart from the phalanx of young women in black who could have arrived for a fashionable wake, looked as if they'd walked in off the street. Here for the beer, eh? He wondered if there were any of them canapés going. He could murder a chicken vol-au-vent.

A designer-stubbled waiter was hovering with a tray of what Alex thought was champagne but which proved to be rather nasty sparkling wine. He took two glasses and placed one in Else's gnarled hand.

Else thanked him without removing the ash-dribbling panatella from her mouth. 'You're a very resourceful young man. You remind me of the late John now what was his name again, dead now of course. You know, the photographer. Now he could get in anywhere, he would charm his way in or bluff his way in. But he was a nasty piece of work, was John it's on the tip of my tongue. I've known so many people at my time of life I forget their names. Yes, a nasty piece of work. But you I think are a nice piece of work.'

'Thank you. So are you,' said Alex woodenly. He wished he could get compliments to trip off his tongue, same as they all seemed to do down here. 'Darling, you're looking absolutely absolute,' they were all saying, mouthing the latest catchphrase. If Alex said anything of that sort back at the Metro they would never stop taking the piss. It was a bit of an art form if you asked him.

They were drifting towards the centre of the room. It was a big room, tall and airy, with a curving glass roof like the Victoria Arcade in Leeds. Alongside it, and overlooking the alleyways behind Frith Street, ran an outside iron walkway, fire escape so Alex supposed, on which loitered a knot of dinner-jacketed figures from what seemed to be a different party, next door probably. Life must be just one long fookin party for this lot.

Else clutched his sleeve excitedly. 'Oh, look! Now that's what he looked like in middle age. They should have used the later portrait, the famous one, but then the other biographies did that, didn't they?'

Alex didn't know what the old trout was rambling on about, except that they had stopped at a long central table stacked with copies of the book they had come to celebrate, and surmounted by a huge cardboard blow-up of its cover. *The Light and the Shade: the Chiaroscuro Life of Augustus John.* Alex had heard of him, just. Didn't know what *chiaro*-whatever-it-was meant, though. Italian, sounded like.

'He did some sketches of me, you know. In the Fitzroy Tavern.'

'So you said.'

'John Minton, I sat for him more than once.' Never heard of him. 'Francis Bacon. Many others. They didn't all climb to the top of the tree, you know, or live high off the hog. Many of my friends died all too young.'

She sounded wistful. She reached out and picked up a copy of the new John biography, spilling a quantity of ash over the frontispiece, an etching of some gypsies. With none-too-clean fingers she leafed through it until she came to a page of pastel drawings, one of them a sepia head and shoulders of a soulful-looking young woman with her hair in a bun. Looked like that young Queen Victoria that you saw on old stamps.

'Here I am. I was very beautiful in those days.'

'Still are,' said Alex gallantly. 'I bet you're a cracker with your teeth in.'

'Epstein was going to do me, you know.' What, shag her, did she mean? Who wouldn't, if that was how she looked? So why didn't he? 'But he died, of course.'

As Else brushed ash from a page, succeeding only in creating a long grey smudge, the book was taken, snatched almost, from her grimy hands by yet another efficient young woman in a black suit with a lapel badge pronouncing her function as Lisa, Sales. She was a bit of a cracker too, in fact So-oh was fuller them. It was a comfort to Alex that if Selby meant to pull while she was down here, there was some stiff competition.

'Excuse me, madam, do you wish to purchase this?'

Without thinking, Alex heard himself say: 'How much is it?'

Well, why the fook not? His hand strayed to what he had learned to call his back sky-rocket. There was two hundred pounds in twenties tucked away in there. Two hundred smackeroos, as Brendan would have called them had he known he'd parted with that much. In fact the extra was not for special services – Christ knew they were special enough as it was, Alex didn't even want to think about that little interlude – but because when it came to peeling off the dosh, which he had done from a wad of readies on the bedside table, Brendan had been too pissed on his own champagne and gin to count properly. And who was Alex to put him right? The bugger had got it, hadn't he, it was practically coming out of his ears.

'Twenty-nine pounds ninety-five, sir.'

Christ on crutches. Oh well, easy come, easy go. His conscience was salved, anyway, if it needed salving.

Clawlike fingers brushed his sleeve. 'You're very kind, young man, very kind indeed. Now perhaps you'd be even kinder and find me another glass of wine.'

Fookin hell. You buy them a thirty quid book but what's even kinder is getting them a glasser wine. Stroll on. Still, they were like that, models.

Wandering off in search of a waiter with a tray of catpiss, Alex caught sight of James Flood, who was talking to Ellis Hugo Bell. Or rather, Ellis Hugo Bell was talking to James Flood.

'We're talking big big big here, Simon,' Bell was saying.

'James,' said James.

'James. We're not talking arthouse crap, can't even get a video release, we're talking major promotion, starry première, the works. But you can't do a thing without seed money.'

James, to his own evident relief, spotted Alex. 'So the wanderer returns. Did you score with our little Jenny, then?'

'That's for you to ask and me to know,' said Alex complacently.

'More to the point,' said Bell, 'did you score with our big Brendan?'

Alex sensed himself blushing again, a habit he'd have to get out of. 'What do you mean by that, exactly?'

'It doesn't always pay to be exact in my business,' said Bell – probably, reflected Alex, the most honest thing he had said all evening. 'But I'll tell you what might interest you. You heard something about this new project of mine, *Kill Me Nicely*, working title. I was just telling Simon here, that's to say Martin here—'

'James,' said James.

'James here, that I'm thinking of cross-fertilising the financing with my other product, *Walk On By*. Every hundred-pound unit of *Walk On By*, once it's in profit, gives you a seed-money cut of *Kill Me Nicely*. Now you heard me talking to Brendan Barton about *Walk On By*. What did you think, speaking frankly?'

Alex took his critical judgement from Brendan. 'Speaking frankly, it sounds like shite to me. But what do I know?'

'Fuck all,' said Ellis Hugo Bell.

'Talking of funding, any more news from the National Lottery?' asked James diplomatically.

Bad-tempered now, Bell snapped: 'Listen, man, if I'd any news from the National Lottery, would I be standing about with this bunch of arseholes drinking horsepiss? I'd be sloshing down the champagne with Brendan. Where is he, anyway?'

'Pissed, I imagine.'

'We know that, but what's keeping him?'

'This very puritan publishing house operates a strict no-drunks policy. They wouldn't even let the author through the doors.'

Feeling far from sober himself, and wilting under the gimlet eye of the black-clad, lapel-badged young woman who had sold him the book, Alex commandeered two glasses of wine and meandered off to rejoin Else. Not only was it horsepiss as Bell had described it – he would convey the term back to Leeds, as a more graphic synonym for catpiss – but it was warm horsepiss by now.

'So very kind of you,' said Else, when he at last located her, for she had now found herself a chair some distance from the book table, where she was browsing through the Augustus John biography, with particular reference to her own quarter-page portrait. 'And now I really must meet the author. Where is the author? He must be here, surely.'

'Rat-arsed.' This was James Flood, who had taken the opportunity to detach himself from the company of Ellis Hugo Bell and follow Alex.

'Inebriated, I should say, Else.' James politely corrected himself for the old lady's benefit.

'Oh, you mean blotto. That's what we used to say when any of us got stinking.'

'Stinking blotto, Else. Apparently he began on the sauce at seven this morning in the Waiters Club. By the time he got to Frith Street this evening he was crawling along on his hands and knees. The law turns up and asks him what he thinks he's doing. "Oh, it'sh all right, oshiffer," he says, "I'm just looking for my car keys." They wouldn't let him in.'

Soddin hell, what a tale he had to tell. He ought to be keeping a blow-by-blow blurry diary. '. . . So the next thing, right, I'm at this book-launch bash, right, and there's this old biddy, famous model she was, posed for all the great artists, August John you name it, and she's like, I've got to meet the author. Turns out he was so pissed they wouldn't let him in. To his own fookin party, can you believe . . .!'

Yes, but could you believe?

'Is that really true, James?'

'I didn't say that, Alex, couldn't swear to it, otherwise I'd print it. But it ought to be, the state he was in when last seen.'

A velvet-scabbarded sheath-knife voice said: 'Then if it isn't true, don't spread it, otherwise it'll finish up in a diary column and you'll find yourself – or more to the point the *Examiner* will find itself, because who gives a fuck about you, Flood – the star witness in a libel action.'

Familiar face – bossy, youngish woman in granny glasses, dressed all in black like every other female around here, who had detached herself from a knot of vaguely well-known-looking people to join James Flood, while at the same time contriving to look as if he were not important enough to join and that she was just passing by.

Yeh yeh, got her in one. Always on some chat-show or other, *Any Questions*, that kinder crap, not that Alex ever watched it but you were supposed to take the odd glance if you were doing media studies. Fuller herself, she was. Right cow. So who the fook was she?

Suddenly nervous, James Flood stammered introductions. 'I don't think you know Alex Singer, Jane. Alex, this is Jane Rich, my editor.'

Jane gave Alex a swift up and down look, half incredulous, half contemptuous, as if he were in need of a good wash the same as Else, before she detachedly asked of James Flood, as one asks the price of an object in a shop: 'Who he?'

Since James was clearly lost for an answer, Alex spoke for himself: 'Nobody.'

Plainly, he should've said: 'A famous sculptor,' or 'An actor out of *Coronation Street*,' or 'Him on the Quaker Oats box, whojer think?' For if Jane had been ignoring him before, she had now, as with the wave of a wand, rendered him completely non-existent. In a low voice to James, not so much to escape being overheard as to ensure that he caught the full force of her venom: 'Without even turning my head an inch in either direction, James, I can spot at least fifteen celebs, every one of whom must have a story for the *Examiner*. So why are you wasting company time chatting up Mr fucking Cellophane?'

Jesus Christ, if this was how women bosses talked to you down in London, and Alex got launched on that media career he was angling for, you definitely would not get him south of the river Aire.

Flushing, James protested: 'Actually, Jane, Alex hasn't got a bad little tale. He's come down from Yorkshire looking for his missing girl-friend.'

'Age?'

'Twenty-one,' volunteered Alex.

'Is he taking the piss, Flood?'

90

Hurriedly, James changed tack: 'And Old Jakie the dead news-vendor being taken for a last pub crawl, that's not a bad yarn.'

'It was in the *Evening Standard* last edition – don't you ever read the papers? Besides, I didn't post you to Soho to write about dead news-vendors. Names – that's what makes news, James. Old Fleet Street saying.'

'How about Ellis Hugo Bell?'

'That wanker?' At least she and Alex agreed about something.

'He's getting a new project together, set right here in Soho. Could be interesting.'

'Did I hear my name?' asked the sole proprietor of Bell Famous Productions, drifting across.

Without even favouring him with one of her viperish looks, Jane said: 'The prat couldn't set up a Punch and Judy show in Soho Square. Now listen to me, James, I'm being very serious. You're here to get stories about modern, vibrant, cutting-edge, state-of-the-art Soho, not wankers, dead newspaper-sellers or—' here Jane flashed a glance of disgust at Else, who was still engrossed in her book, or more particularly the quarter-page sketch of herself when young '—old crones who were artists' models in the year dot. Her Soho's dead, gone, *finito*. Get on the case, Flood, or get off the pot. Never forget you're on three months' trial, now move. I'm off to the Grouch.'

And off she – it was the only word for it – flounced. But no, looking after her retreating figure – good class bum, that, thought Alex – there was a better word, marched. Off she marched, head held high, swinging her arms from side to side, as if accompanied by the band of the Coldstream Guards.

Alex whistled under his breath. 'You've got a right goer there, James old lad.'

'You can say that again.'

'Does she – er – give a turn?'

'Not with me she doesn't.'

'Only she looks as if she's up for it. Needs one too, ask me. Calm her down a bit.'

'Swallow you for breakfast and spit the pips out,' said Ellis Hugo Bell.

James Flood, who had been looking pensive, piped up, out of a separate conversation he was holding with himself, 'I never knew that.'

'Wossat, kidder?'

'That I was on three months' trial. No one ever told me.'

'Know what they say, Jas,' said Alex philosophically. 'You learn something new every—' He broke off with a 'Jesus H. Christ!' of pain cross-hatched with surprise as a thick wad of paper hurtled down from the skylight and smote him between the shoulder-blades before slithering to the floor. Staggering to his knees, Alex retrieved what proved to be a soiled bundle of typewritten manuscript. *Freeze When You Say That*, by Kim Grizzard.

Meanwhile all eyes were directed by a strangulated cry of 'Let me get at the bastard, you bastardising bastards!' from the iron walkway running alongside the glass roof, where Kim, at a tipped-open skylight window, was struggling with two of the dinner-jacketed partygoers who had been taking the air.

All eyes particularly those of Ellis Hugo Bell. With an exclamation of 'Shit wrapped in Cellophane!' he was bounding out of the room even as Grizzard, wrenching himself free, leaped through the skylight and crashed down on to the book table – a collapsible trestle affair, as it

92

proved, which duly collapsed, scattering volumes of the *Chiaroscuro Life of Augustus John* in all directions, and bringing down the cardboard blow-up of the book cover, which missed Else by inches.

'When this was the Old Vienna Restaurant, long before it became whatever it is now,' rambled Else imperturbably to no one in particular, 'students from the St Martin's School of Art used to do that for a bet. That was when you could get a Wiener schnitzel and an apfelstrudel to follow, with half a bottle of Tyrol wine for nine and sixpence. Excellent coffee, I remember. Is that young man all right?'

Grizzard was in fact winded but otherwise in better shape than he was going to be after the managerial-type-cum-bouncer had manhandled him roughly out of the wreckage of the book table and frogmarched him off the premises.

'That should give you a headline, kidder,' said Alex, as a subdued Kim Grizzard was led out. 'Even that stupid cow you work for should see that.'

'What's the story?' asked James Flood gloomily. 'Man jumps through skylight, so what? I'll give it to *Private Eye*.'

Alex found himself still clutching the battered manuscript of *Freeze When You Say That*. 'Won't he be wanting this?'

'Leave it down at reception,' advised James. 'Or get Else to drop it in on her way out – she seems to be just leaving.'

As indeed Else just was, escorted by the senior greeter who must have come up to see what the commotion was about.

'Come along, Else, you've seen all there is to see.'

'I expect you're right, if the author isn't going to be here. Would you call me a cab, dear?'

'I don't think we could find one to take you, Else.'

Alex saw that a line of tiny droplets led back to the chair where Else had been sitting. Its red velvet seat was deeply stained and water still dribbled through it to form a little puddle on the parquet floor.

'Now you must give me a moment to say goodbye to my young man,' said damp old Else. Putting a grubby hand in his: 'You were very kind to give me this book and I shall treasure it. If I ever write my memoirs, young man, you must come to my publisher's party and I shall sign you a copy. In the meantime I have something for you.'

She rummaged in her worn tapestry handbag and fished out a creased invitation card. It was for the Soho Ball at the Café Royal, admit two. 'They send me a card every year, yet when I turn up they refuse to let me in. It's very curious. Now I want you to have this and take your young lady along and have a most enjoyable evening. I used to have supper at the Café Royal three or four times a week, you know.'

Alex saw that the invitation was for the following evening, when he would be sitting in an articulated rhubarb truck and heading for South Higginshaw. Anyway, it was black tie. But there was no point in arguing the toss with the old biddy. He'd give the invite away. Or did it have a saleable value? Ask his new mate James.

'Ta very much, Else. I'd take you if I could.' He lunged at the least begrimed furrow on her raddled cheek and gave her a swift peck.

'Now I really must be toddling along. No, don't tell me your name' – he hadn't been about to. 'I never wanted to know the names of my lovers unless they were famous. A lesson I learned from Nina Hamnett. Have you heard of Nina Hamnett?'

'Don't think so.'

'Come along, Else.'

'In a moment, my dear, you must let me finish my little story. She was a celebrated model in her day. We both were. And one afternoon in the Gargoyle Club Augustus John asked her why she always went with sailors. And do you know what her reply was?'

'Else, you must leave.'

'No, her reply was, "Because they sail away next morning. Yes, because they sail away next morning."'

Could be So-oh's motter, that, reflected Alex, as Else allowed herself to be led away at last.

At the top of the stairs Else was handed over to the junior greeter and the senior greeter returned to the now restored book table. A familiar figure hovered behind her.

No, not him, not the prat who seemed to spend all his time wandering around Soho boring for Britain to anyone who would listen about who used to live hereabouts a hundred years ago. No, not Len Gates: Alex had already clocked him lurking, and had taken care to keep out of his way. But beyond Len, a flash of green, where all the other lasses were wearing black. And Alex could almost smell her perfume, although he knew he couldn't really, not at this distance, and anyway, she was gone. But not before the flash of green had been supplemented by a flashing smile in his direction. An inviting one? Invitation to what? Christine, that was her name, wasn't it?

The senior greeter tapped on a wine glass for attention with a classy-looking pen. Alex didn't know much about pens, fact he had never seen one that didn't look as if it had come in an appeal fund envelope from Save the Children, but this one was classy, slimline, gold, could be. He wondered, in passing, if the senior greeter with those big challenging knockers below the power shoulders was available. Forgerrit, kidder, outer your league. That Christine had brought on a case of the passing hots, that was the trouble.

'Ladies and gentlemen, thank you for taking time out from your busy schedules to celebrate this new and fascinating biography of one of this century's leading artists and certainly among its most colourful figures, Augustus John. Unfortunately the author is unfortunately indisposed and so unfortunately he cannot be with us tonight, but fortunately –' here the greeter seemed to do a rapid finger-count on her adverbs and reached for a synonym – 'happily, ladies and gentlemen, we have a gentleman here, I'm sure already known to many of you, who can happily tell us all we need to know about the colourful, *chiaroscuro* life of Augustus John. Ladies and gentlemen, the Sage of Soho, Mr Len Gates.'

Len stepped forward, producing a formidable sheaf of notes, and was about to mount the chair recently vacated by Else when he noted its damp condition. Instead, beckoning his audience forward, he addressed it from ground level.

'Ladies and gentlemen, thank you very much, the late Mr Augustus Edwin John, ARA, whether as colourist or draughtsman, as portrait painter *par excellence* or landscapist, ranked with the great masters. Born at Tenby, Wales, on January four 1878 he studied at the Slade School. Whilst he was awarded the Order of Merit in 1942, he was never to be honoured with a knighthood, possibly on account of a somewhat raffish lifestyle here in Soho . . .'

Alex felt an elbow in his ribs as James jerked his head towards the exit, at the same time executing a knife and fork pantomime with his hands. The pair sidled out.

5

Baldini's in Romilly Street was one of the last of the old family-run restaurants in Soho. Old Jakie, now being conveyed in state past its red-painted frontage on his way from the Crown and Two Chairmen to the Coach and Horses, would have remembered delivering a daily churn of milk there from the Welsh Dairy two doors along where he worked as a boy. The fact that he would have been lying, in that Baldini's went back only as far as 1951 – for ancient Soho restaurants were these days more recent than they were – was neither here nor there. It could not be long now before Baldini's became another branch of Starbucks. Unknown to its dwindling band of regulars, and certainly unknown to James Flood, Soho correspondent of the *London Examiner*, the deeds had already exchanged hands and the widowed Mrs Powolny, the last of her line, was looking at bungalows in Hove.

Left to himself, Alex would have preferred a Chinese or a vindaloo. Baldini's, he surmised, would be Eye-tie. He wasn't all that struck on spag bollox-knees, but on the other hand he was in with a chance of James standing treat. They were on exes, as he understood it, these journos.

The Dutch-print-looking dark interior of the small restaurant, lit only by Chianti-bottle table lamps with exotic hotel labels pasted over their mock-parchment shades, was divided into banquette-lined tall-backed wooden booths, so that it was impossible to see whether the place was full or empty. Good place for a snog, judged Alex, if a bit on the suicidal side.

Mrs Powolny herself, a ramrod-backed middle-aged lady dressed in black like all the other women round here – must be flavour of the month, reckoned Alex – came forward to greet them. In fact, apart from a morose-looking cross-eyed waiter standing by a serving hatch in a resigned sort of way, as if he were a victim of low expectations from the establishment he worked for, there seemed to be no other staff.

'Two, was it? Have you booked?'

Alex saw James's face fall. On the way round from Silhouettes he had rather given the impression that he was known here, that he would be given the best table and be fawned over.

Obviously trying to save face he said heartily: 'Good evening, Mrs Powolny, James Flood of the *Examiner*.' A proffered peck on the cheek was rejected by a backwards flinch as if he suffered from halitosis. 'No, we don't have a reservation as it happens on this occasion, but I'm sure you can squeeze us in as you usually do.'

Mrs Powolny looked doubtfully about the room, at the same time shaking her head, as if, with the best will in the world, she would be unable to accommodate Prince Charles himself if he walked through the door without having booked a table. What the fook did she think she was playing at? The place was blurry empty.

'Waitah!'

No, the place blurry wasn't. The booming voice from the farthermost booth was an all-too-familiar one. 'Is this duck on its way or is the chef still trying to wring the bugger's neck? One only asks.'

'Iss on ees way, Meester Brendan Barton sair.'

'About bloody time. And give us some more wine, would you, chop chop? We haven't taken a vow of abstinence, you know, or at least I haven't. More Pellegrino for Mr Dance.'

'Yes, sair, Meester Brendan Barton, right away, sair.'

'Follow me,' said Mrs Powolny, as if granting James and Alex an audience with some luminary, and led them past three empty booths on either side of a central aisle to the one at the end of the room that was directly opposite Brendan Barton's table, presumably on the principle that if you crowd your customers together the room looks busier, or anyway the waiter has less far to walk.

Brendan Barton, with foam flecking his lips and the sweat running down his beetroot face, was by now so drunk that he looked as if he might have a seizure. His companion, quietly if ostentatiously dressed – the quietness of his grey-stripe flannel suit was insistent about making its point – and with a moustache that looked as if it had a barber in to trim it each morning (which was in fact the case) was as sober as Brendan was drunk.

Alex had been rather hoping to go through his remaining time in Soho without setting eyes on Brendan Barton again. He feared that he was looking sheepish. Against that, he thought there was a good case for Brendan looking so too. But Brendan, for his part, showed no sign of recognising either Alex or James. It seemed probable, in his present state, that he wouldn't even have recognised his own mother.

James Flood's nod went unacknowledged. He tried – as a journalist, James had steeled himself to become a compulsive greeter – nodding at Brendan's guest.

'Do I know you, remind me?' asked Stephan Dance.

'James Flood, *London Examiner*, Mr Dance,' said James sycophantically. 'We have met. Here and elsewhere.'

'Yes,' said Dance. 'And the answer's still no.'

'The answer to what question, Mr Dance?'

'*London Examiner*, yes I know. You're about to ask me how's business. If I say terrific, it'll be "Clampdown on Sex Shops Fails To Curb Vice King". If I say terrible, it's "Sex Shop Clampdown Curbs Vice King". How can I win? So the answer's no, no interviews.'

'Point taken, Mr Dance, but apart from that, how's business?' asked James – rather cheekily, it seemed to Alex, given that this Mr Dance looked as if he carried an open razor or knew someone who did. Alex had seen his quota of old J. Arthur Rank movies where the villains were known to the law as Chummy and carried chivs. Bit old for the gaunt-faced Dirk Bogarde part was this Mr Dance, but you never knew.

'Ticking over,' said Stephan Dance, sipping his Pellegrino. 'But that's off the record.'

'Waitah!'

Alex had never come across a porn king before. Did they have them in Leeds? Must do, he supposed. Shouldn't he have a blonde bimbo on his arm? And what was he doing out with Brendan Barton? Supplying him with kinky pix, that would be it. Yeh yeh, being the public personality that he was, Brendan couldn't risk going into a dodgy bookshop, so he would deal personally with this Mr Dance, one to one. Right, got it. It was like wunner the big stores staying open just for someone like Madonna to do her shopping.

'Waitah! Another bottle of your seven pounds fifty pee house white, how many more fucking times?'

'We don' have no seven fifty house white, Meester Brendan Barton sair.'

'Yes you do, you charge whatever it is you charge for it.'

That sounded a bit lame to Alex, especially since he'd already heard the joke twice today. Brendan really was well away, he could barely speak, let alone deliver punchlines.

The cross-eyed waiter, on his way back to the serving hatch, tossed two menus at James, his distorted aim being such that one landed on the floor and the other in Alex's lap.

'No soup,' counselled the waiter in passing.

Scanning his menu Alex grumbled: 'There must be *some* kinder blurry soup, which one does he mean?' He could've given a bowl of minestrone a right seeing-to after a day of privation. Then there was supposed to be *zuppa di pesce, stracciatella, zuppa pavese*, what was he talking about, no fookin soup?

'So which of these is off, mate?' he asked, as the waiter scurried back with Brendan's bottle of house white.

'Nossing is off, sair. Jus' so long as you don' mind eating your soup wiz a fork.'

This was definitely going to be one for the lads once Alex had worked out what was going on. He turned to James for enlightenment.

As if explaining everything, James said: 'He doesn't mean no soup, he means no soup spoons.'

Stephan Dance leaned across while the waiter opened Brendan's bottle – the latest of a good number, at a guess. 'Don't quote me, laddie, but if that happened in my line of business there'd be shop managers walking around this patch with no hands.' To the waiter he said: 'It's that Guido who's done the runner, isn't it?'

'Yes, sair, Meester Stephan Dance, sair. He starts at Pizza Heaven tomorrow, sair. I tell him a hundert times, iss a pizza place, they don' serve soup, what they want with soup spoons, take some coffee spoons, but no, he won't listen, Meester Stephan Dance sair.'

'Whereas you yourself are a model of attentiveness?' barked Brendan Barton, coming out of a light doze.

'At all times, Meester Brendan Barton sair,' smirked the waiter.

'So to reiterate a previous and frequently asked question, where the fuck is my fucking duck?'

'Iss on iss way, Meester Brendan Barton.'

'Dowry,' said James to Alex, by way of further explanation of the soup-spoon theme.

'Bung,' expanded Stephan Dance.

'You've lost me, sorry,' said Alex, mystified. Mebbe not one for the lads after all, he didn't have the first idea what they were rabbiting on about.

Brendan Barton, to claim Alex's attention, lurched across Stephan Dance, thereby knocking over Dance's bottle of Pellegrino and spilling most of it down his trousers. In anyone else, was Alex's guess, the incident could well have led to a charge of grievous bodily harm, perhaps involving the serrated knife which Dance had instinctively grabbed. But the porn-shop king merely assumed a resigned expression and reached for a napkin. That Brendan Barton must be a good customer.

'Read my book, you ignorant Yorkshire tyke,' boomed Brendan across to Alex. '*Soho Nights*, now sadly out of print. I in turn stole the story from *Soho Days* by Lieutenant Colonel Newnham Davies, who very probably made it up himself. Gastronomic critic of the old *Pall Mall Gazette*, known as the Dwarf of Blood.'

'What was he called that for?' asked Alex, in the interest of garnering research for the lads.

'Leave it, son,' advised Stephan Dance, leaning over and waving a cautionary knife. 'He'll tell you what he wants to tell you. What he don't want to tell you, he won't tell you. It's how we are, is that right or isn't it, James?'

'It's right,' mumbled James obediently, in a cowed way. And Alex sensed, for the first time in this curious catchment area, menace. No one had done anything to him. No one had threatened him. But it was there, he now grasped, and rendered portable by the likes of the Pellegrino-sipping Stephan Dance.

'To answer your extremely boring question,' said Brendan Barton, 'the Dwarf of Blood was, as you could have worked out in your own pinpoint head in ten seconds, a *nom de plume* or if I have to spell that out a pen name. *Pen name!*' he emphasised, with elephantine patience. 'And the story he told was that in the very old days when all these little restaurants were owned by immigrant families from Italy and Greece or wherever, it was the done thing when you changed your job as a waiter or commis chef or whatever to take to your next place a dowry of cutlery or plates or cups and saucers or whatever you could get away with, am I losing you as an audience?'

'Not at all,' said Alex politely.

'Because you see they couldn't afford to stock up on cutlery and crockery themselves. So the Dwarf of Blood having planted the tale, it became a what's the word I'm looking for, tradition, custom, old Soho ritual, load of bollox, what the fuck is this supposed to be?'

The last segment of Brendan's words was addressed to the cross-eyed waiter, who had placed in his approximate vicinity a side dish of admittedly shrivelled petits pois to accompany his main dish of duck à l'orange. Brendan prodded the metal dish with a fork and reiterated: 'I say, what is this green heap of shit, waitah?'

You would never get away with this in Leeds, not

anywhere. The waiter, plainly containing himself, said in a strained voice: 'Issa petits pois you ordaired, Meester Brendan Barton sair.'

Brendan flung down his fork with such force that a splash of green mush reached Stephan Dance's right sleeve. Another capital offence in Alex's view.

'These are not petits pois, you scoundrel, these are the pellets you shot the fucking duck with.'

Sodding hell fire, he was well out of order there. The cross-eyed waiter, lower lip trembling, stared at Stephan Dance in a hurt spaniel sort of way, in the belief that he was staring at Brendan Barton.

'Meester Brendan Barton sair, in thirty-five years I am at Baldini's as a waiter, nevair have I been spoken to in such a way, if I may say so, sair.'

Brendan triumphantly thumped the table, causing some of the offending petits pois to jump out of their dish and roll about the tablecloth like the pellets he claimed they were. 'You've worked in the same establishment for thirty-five years and you're still a lousy waiter. I'm not fucking surprised, when you serve used ammunition as a vegetable!'

That was enough for the waiter. Crossed eyes brimming with tears, he stumbled off through a green baize door evidently leading down to the kitchen.

'You don't think he's taken offence, do you, Brendan?' murmured Stephan Dance, with mock concern.

'If he hasn't, he's even more insensitive than I thought,' snarled Brendan, swigging down a whole glass of wine in one gulp, with the result that for the next few moments the small restaurant reverberated with loud hiccoughs.

The green baize door swung open forcefully as, grim-faced, Mrs Powolny marched out to Brendan's table. 'I'm very sorry, Mr Barton, but I'm going to have to ask you to leave. You'll have to excuse me, Mr Dance, but good waiters are hard to find, I can't have Mr Barton upsetting my staff every time he comes in, I'm very sorry but I don't care who he is.'

'He'll get over it, woman,' rumbled Brendan, fishing in his trouser pockets. He produced the familiar, to Alex, wad of twenty-pound notes and peeled one off. 'Here, give him this and tell him if he can't take a joke he shouldn't have joined.'

Mrs Powolny declined the money. 'Yes, and how many times have we heard you come out with that one, Mr Barton? But I'm afraid this time the joke's on you. He's gone. He's walked out.'

'Oh, yes?' said Brendan affably. 'Did he take the cutlery?'

Right, yeh yeh yeh, this was all very entertaining and Alex would have to remember that line about did he take the cutlery, but on the other hand he was starving hungry.

'Any chance of a steak and chips, luv?' he asked plaintively, as Mrs Powolny turned on her heel.

'I'm sorry, sir, we're closing.'

'What about a doggy bag for the duck?' roared Brendan after her, but she was already barging through the green baize door.

'Come on, Brendan, let's have it away on our toes to Mr Wong's in Wardour Street,' persuaded Stephan Dance.

Allowing Dance to help him to his feet, Brendan Barton found himself still clutching his wad of twenty-pound notes. He transferred his gaze from the bundle of notes to Alex, at the same time trading in the glance for a glare.

'Oh, yes! Reminds me. That young bugger there owes me fifty pounds.'

Alex felt himself going white, but decided on a policy of silence.

'Talking to you, son,' prompted Stephan Dance politely.

'Don't know what he's on about,' mumbled Alex. He would be sweating in a minute. Oh, Christ, don't let him sweat.

'You allowed me to overcharge myself,' said Brendan, swaying. 'The agreement was a hundred to a hundred and fifty, according to the quality of the service. I have no complaints against the service, that I'll grant you, young feller-me-lad, but taking advantage of my condition, that's to say rat-arsed, you went off with two hundred smackeroos.'

Alex was aghast. The prat was babbling away as if the whole world knew his business. And here was he, Alex, sitting next to a fookin reporter from the fookin press. Not, he had to acknowledge, that James Flood looked that much interested. But mebbe he wasn't as good a reporter as all that.

Ludicrously trying to keep his voice down, since there was nothing he might say in whatever undertone he could manage that would not be heard by the others present, he said – hissed, almost: 'I thought you didn't want that stuff to get about.'

'Oh, do be your age, sunshine, don't you ever read your *Private Eye*? I'm notorious. Bottoms-up Brendan, I'm known as, I thought everyone knew that. What I didn't want the world and his wife to know was that, mistakenly as it now seems, I was paying you over top whack if you'll excuse the expression. Seventy-five is the going rate, I paid you double the going rate for a double blessing, so to speak, but then you took me for a further fifty which is unforgivable. Poppy up.'

Jesus, had the bugger no shame? Apparently not. He was standing with his outstretched palm level with Stephan Dance's waistline, which made it worse.

'Sorry, Brendan, I was a bit pissed. I wasn't counting.'

'Nevertheless.'

106

'If you pay the gentleman,' said Stephan Dance, 'we can all leave in an orderly manner.'

What the alternative was to leaving in an orderly manner he didn't specify, but there was no doubt in Alex's mind that there was one. Nevertheless, he bluffed: 'But I don't have it on me.' After all, so all right, he'd been dropped two hundred, but thirty of that had already gone on that old bat's book, another fifty back to Brendan would take it down to a hundred and twenty, and where did a hundred and twenty go in this fookin town? It was only just after ten.

'Get it,' suggested Stephan Dance, with chilling firmness. He felt in his top pocket for a visiting card. 'Fetch it round here.' *Eve's Erotica. Adult video's – book's – mag's. Sale or rent.* 'Open till midnight,' added the porn king helpfully.

'What if I haven't got it by then?' asked Alex brashly.

'My son, you'll turn into a pumpkin,' said Stephan Dance, and sounded as if he meant it. 'Off we jolly go, Brendan.'

In a near-zombie trance, Brendan Barton suffered himself to be led out. Alex was left alone with James. Mrs Powolny reappeared, in her outdoor coat, and pointedly began to turn off table lamps.

'Don't forget this,' said James as they rose. It was the scruffed-up manuscript of *Freeze When You Say That*, by Kim Grizzard.

Oh, shit. Alex had tried to leave it with the receptionist over at Silhouettes, but she had not unreasonably declined to take possession of it on the basis that Kim Grizzard was now barred from the restaurant for life and beyond.

'Try not to lose it,' advised James. 'You're in enough doo-doo as it is.'

As they passed out into Romilly Street Alex asked: 'That bollox about soup spoons – were they pulling our plonkers or what?'

The Soho correspondent of the *London Examiner* shrugged. 'It doesn't do to question what's bollox and what's not around here. Especially in my job, such as it is.'

Across the street Len Gates, furled umbrella raised so that he could be identified by stragglers, had gathered another small band of tourists about him in a pool of lamplight.

'Jesus Christ, doesn't he ever stop?' said Alex. 'I wonder he doesn't get blurry laryngitis.'

'This is his ghost walk,' explained James. 'Very popular, I gather. Conducted tour of all the haunted spots in Soho.'

'Stuff me! How many are there supposed to be, then?'

'Depends on the number of punters and the state of the weather.'

They meandered across Romilly Street, within hailing distance of Len's braying voice but beyond the range of his collecting hat.

'Ladies and gentlemen, the excellent Pizza Plaza before you now was in days gone by a very very famous seafood house known as Strong's Fish Restaurant. And if you would look upwards, you will see set into the wall the ceramic lobster which was the emblem, the logo as it would nowadays be termed, of the Strong family's little chain of restaurants.

'Now, ladies and gentlemen, the last Mr Strong who ran this very restaurant, used to tell this story himself. That when he was manager here he regularly had the experience of finding himself, in the early hours, sprawled at the foot of the very steep flight of cellar steps, his explanation being that he was deliberately pushed down them. By whom, ladies and gentlemen? Mr Strong always maintained that it was the shade of a certain Mrs Kark who had been manageress before the Strong family took the establishment over, and that this was her way of paying him out after passing to the other side. A more mundane explanation was that Mr Strong was frequently to be seen in liquor. Who is to say? Only the ghosts of Soho know.'

'Does he make this stuff up as he goes along?' asked Alex as they moved on towards the Coach and Horses.

'Put it this way,' said James Flood. 'The last time I heard him spin that yarn he was standing outside what used to be the old Hungaria restaurant in Coventry Street, and the ghost was an old waiter who'd been fired and was then run over by a cab on his way across to Lyons' Corner House.'

'Oh, yes, and did he take the cutlery?' asked Alex, echoing Brendan Barton.

'Well may you ask.'

'Now before we move on to the site of the old Royalty Theatre and the ghost of its late owner Fanny Kelly, ladies and gentlemen, let me draw your attention back to the Strong family's lobster emblem on the wall there. Those of you who have vouchers for luncheon at the Mermaid Room of the Cambridge Eurotel tomorrow may care to notice that many of the fish forks in that restaurant are stamped with that very same lobster emblem. Now how did those fish forks come to be transferred from what was Strong's seafood house to the Mermaid Room? Thereby, ladies and gentlemen, hangs a tale . . .'

6

Starting at the Coach and Horses, they went on to the French House, the Pillars of Hercules, the Blue Posts, the Three Greyhounds and the Admiral Duncan in a zigzagging pub crawl that ended up at the Wellington Arms off Shaftesbury Avenue at near closing time.

They missed Old Jakie at the Coach but caught up with him at the Wellington, where the two flymen seemed to be conducting something of an impromptu funeral service on Quaker lines. After some stumbled tributes – 'He was a good mate, he'd give you the coat off his back' and suchlike maudlin sentiments – someone suggested a hymn. Gathered around Old Jakie, whose makeshift bier was resting across two pub tables, the congregation began a ragged rendering of 'For Those In Peril On The Sea,' taking the first flyman's word for it, on little evidence, that their man had served briefly in the Merchant Navy in the course of his varied career.

The singsong was brought to a trailing halt by the fact that few present knew all the words, and by the landlord pointing out that he did not have a music licence and anyway it was past drinking-up time. When last seen by Alex and James, the two flymen were preparing to escort Old Jakie to the Shamrock Club in Camden Town, where although not a member and not even Irish, he had always been made most welcome.

After the Wellington, James took Alex to a drinking

club he knew, Kemble's in Compton's Yard at the back of Old Compton Street, identical in all respects to the New Kismet at the end of Frith Place around the corner, except that it was upstairs where the New Kismet was downstairs, and in place of the short-tempered Mabel there was an even more short-tempered personage named Robbie, who looked like, and indeed was, a podgy, quite well-known middle-aged bit player Alex had seen on one of the television soaps. This was no time, however, to ask for Robbie's autograph (and why hadn't he got Brendan Barton's and Jenny Wise's while they were going? Prat, Singer), for he was engaged in haranguing the club's only other customer – was there a rule against more than one member using wunner these dumps at any given time, then? Mebbe it was a fire regulation – who was a very drunken Ellis Hugo Bell of Bell Famous Productions Ltd.

'How would you like it,' the irascible Robbie was chuntering, 'if I rang your doorbell and said, "Ho, I was just passing, Mr Bell, so you won't mind if I drop in for a quick pee, I'm sure."'

'For Christ's sake, Robbie, where else can I get a slash at this time of night?'

'I'm sure I don't know, but this isn't a public urinal,' said Robbie. 'You're not a member and your cock's certainly not a member, except in the anatomical sense, so I suggest you go piss it out wherever you soaked it up.'

'But all the pubs are closed by now, Robbie.'

'Tough titty. Besides, there's only one bog here as you know, and it's in use.'

'And I'm next,' chimed in James Flood, with a mischievous smirk at Bell's discomfiture.

But the director of Bell Famous Productions smote his forehead in inspiration. 'You two have just given me the most brill idea. I tell you – you know my *Walk On By* project?'

'Oh, Gawd, she's off,' sighed Robbie. 'No shoptalk in the mess, would you mind?'

'How would it be,' pursued Bell, 'if instead of setting up my camera in a café doorway, I set it up outside your bog?'

'Inside the bog would be more interesting,' said Robbie.

'No, like I'm serious, man. Also I'm peeing myself,' Bell remembered. 'Who the hell have you got in there, anyway?'

'Kim Grizzard,' said Robbie, with the studied casualness that usually comes with looking at one's nails.

The effect was gratifying. 'Jesus hopping Christ! I wasn't here, all right?'

Bell cleared the room in two strides and made for the stairs with such haste that he could be heard half falling down them.

A saturnine chuckle from Robbie. 'Well, at least he'll have got what he came in for.'

Alex, in this town always ready to supply a feedline if someone could come up with a punchline to tell the lads back at the Metro, prompted: 'What's that, then?'

'He came in for a slash and he'll definitely have pissed himself on the way out.'

'Is that really Kim Grizzard in there?' asked James.

'No, but it could well have been. He was in not half an hour ago, baying for Bell's liver and lights.'

Oh, shite. Because it wouldn't only be Bell's liver and lights the bugger would be baying for. *Freeze When You Say That*. What had Alex done with the manuscript? He had had it when he and James left Baldini's and now he didn't, it was as simple as that. No use trying to retrace his steps – all the pubs would be closed by now. No use, either, asking James to use his influence with the licensees, if any influence he had which Alex begged leave to doubt. James had already announced, upon allowing him the privilege of buying a last double brandy each, that he had to check in at the Groucho Club to report to his boss that he had nothing to report. Shite and double shite. And in any case, as James now reminded him upon knocking back his brandy, it was coming up to ten minutes before midnight, the hour at which Stephan Dance had threatened to have him turned into a pumpkin if he didn't come up with Brendan Barton's fifty pounds. Shite and triple shite.

The lavatory cistern flushed and who should emerge but old Else, clutching the Augustus John biography that Alex had bought for her.

'I'm sorry if I've kept anyone waiting,' said Else to the room at large, such as it was, 'but I've been so engrossed in this book that someone kindly gave me.' She showed no sign of recognising her benefactor. Ta very much, thought Alex, not without bitterness. 'It's all about the late Augustus John, him with his golden ear-rings. Of course, he painted a good many gypsies, you know.'

'Don't sit on that bar stool, dear, it's taken!' said – yelped, almost – Robbie.

'There's a mention in here of how whenever he entered the Café Royal, all the art students from the Slade School who were drinking in the old Domino Room would rise to their feet out of respect. Now that wouldn't happen nowadays, would it, Robbie, because what Slade School student could afford to drink at the Café Royal at today's prices?'

'Yes, dear, but don't sit on the bar stool, the cat doesn't like it.'

'I could sit on a tea-towel,' volunteered the incontinent Else helpfully. 'In any case, I've only just been, so an accident is most unlikely. He sketched me more than once, you know. Rothenstein considered him a genius, and Sargent called him the greatest draughtsman since the Renaissance. Let me just read you this passage, if I can find it.'

'Not from a sitting position, dear, it'll play your back up. Stand up straight and use the bar stool as a lectern.'

James had given Alex a sharp tap on the ankle and nudged him towards the door. As they went down the stairs he said: 'I won't ask you into the lioness's den because she tends to get embarrassing after midnight. But as soon as she's spat the pips out you'll find me down in Gerry's Club licking my wounds, if you feel like a nightcap. Anyone'll tell you where it is.'

Who anyone? wondered Alex, as James Flood hurried off to dance attendance upon his editor at the Groucho. Anyone who knew their way around Soho, of course. If they didn't know, you were accosting the wrong anyone.

He had to eat something. He turned into Old Compton Street and took his bearings, or tried to. The night was busy, the atmosphere tensed-up, tingling with electricity. Could be storm clouds brewing, could be the excitement generated by a street mob-full of people, some of them sipping caffè latte at the pavement tables, but most of them hurrying along as if going somewhere, or waiting at the corners for non-appearing black cabs. Occasionally a couple would climb into an illicitly cruising minicab. A white stretch limo with darkened windows edged slowly along the street. Yeh yeh yeh yeh yeh, they had wunner them in Leeds. Crowds gathered when it pulled up at the Majestick nightclub in City Square, in the hope that someone like Michael Jackson must be in it. They were disappointed when it disgorged a gaggle of giggling girlies and sheepishly grinning laddoes who'd all chipped in for a ride up from Burley-in-Wharfedale or somewhere. But this being down here, mebbe it really was Michael Jackson or somebody.

Whoever, Alex could not understand where everyone was going. Soho was supposed to be where the action was, where it was all at as the old phrase had it, yet they were all darting off somewhere else like rabbits down a hole. Mebbe at this timer night Soho wasn't where it was all going on after all. Could be they were larging it in Covent Garden, King's Road, Camden Lock would it be? – wunner them places, anyway. And mebbe that explained why Selby was nowhere to be found.

Following the human tide that was washing out of Old Compton Street and its environs, cross-current with another tide swilling in from Shaftesbury Avenue and Charing Cross Road, Alex was reminded of Venice. Not that he'd ever set foot in Venice but he'd seen video footage of it and the ambience, as he'd heard it called, was similar. Same vibrancy, though of course without the canals.

He found himself just round from Cambridge Circus, at a fast-food joint called the Yankee Doodle Diner. Yeh yeh, franchise job, there were a coupler them in Leeds, same decor, same menu, same T-shirts on the waiters – Cocksuckin Cowgirls, the slogan was – exact replica in fact. Not the same prices, though, not by a long chalk. He perched at the end of a chrome horseshoe bar and ordered. 'I'll get a tuna melt, wet fries, Diet Coke float.' Dead funny, he thought as he waited. Only been down here a day and already he was talking like a blurry Londoner. But was he? Alex realised that in the equivalent establishment on Leeds Bridge he would have phrased his order in the same words, with the same off-Yankee intonation. Everybody talked the same these days, he reckoned, except that they used a different language to suit different venues. Patois, that was the word. And upspeak, as James had told him the expression was? How half these young women in black talked? As if they were asking a question? As if they'd once been to New York? He'd remember all this, bung it in an essay sometime.

A couple of seats along some bird was yakking away on her mobile. '. . . So he's like, "Get your act together for Chrissake," and I'm like, "I'm totally arsed with this liner talk," and he's like, "I'm telling you, babe", so I'm like, "Fuck you . . ."' Jesus Christ, they were total pants, summer these women you got down here. But Alex had been prompted to tug his own mobile out of his shirt pocket.

A game plan was forming in Alex's by now somewhat addled mind. Get Selby's mate Vicky in Leeds on the blower. He had been in friggin Soho over five friggin hours and there was no sign of Selby. So where was she? Was she coming out of her hideyhole or not? If not, sod her. He would have it away on his toes, as Stephan Dance would have put it, right out of Soho. Sod Brendan Barton and his fifty quid. Sod Stephan Dance – his porn emporium would have long closed by now, anyway, and he would have crawled back down whatever hole he lived in. Unless he was lurking in wunner them clubs. But Alex wouldn't be here. And sod Kim Grizzard and his blurry manuscript. With a hundred and seventy quid in his pocket – well, far less than that by now, it must be nearer a hundred and thirty after that mad pub crawl with James Flood, who for someone supposedly on exes put his hand in his pocket less than often, and the big mistake of going on to large brandies; but it was still more cash than he had ever seen in cash.

There must be an all-night coach service to Leeds, if he could find out where it went from. Victoria, would it be, wherever Victoria was? Away on his toes.

Unless . . . But there was no reply from Vicky. Must be out clubbing, this timer night. Shite. All right, he'd give it an hour. Meanwhile he'd find out where this Gerry's Club was, where James Flood reckoned he was going to be.

A clap of thunder welcomed him back into Cambridge Circus, where a three-card-trick hustler and his drummer, which Alex happened to know was the term for the guy who was supposed to drum up trade by pretending to put a bet on and winning, had set up their orange-box stall outside the theatre. Nah nah nah, you didn't catch Alex like that, not born yesterday. He'd watch for a coupler minutes, though. Coupler gullible tourists, wanted to chuck their dosh down the toilet. Middle card they were both on, in tenners. Total prats. Fookin hell, the middle card came up and they were paid out. Yeh yeh yeh, though, but it was only a come-on, wasn't it? Next time round they'd push the betting up to twenty and go down. They pushed the betting up to twenty and came up. Alex began to finger the bundle of notes in his trouser pocket.

Total prat that he was himself, he had lost fifty pounds by the time another crack of thunder, and a spattering of raindrops the size of the dollar pancakes he'd seen being served at the Yankee Doodle Diner, drove him back along Moor Street, the conduit to Soho.

When the actual downpour came – stair-rods, you were talking about – he found a deep-set doorway to scuttle into. With its heavy, uncompromising door, it looked like a club of some kind. Gerry's? No: the small brass plate over the Ansaphone buzzer you had to press to gain admission identified it as the Transylvania Club, members only. He wondered idly what kind of a joint it was.

He was offered a clue in the shape of a black cab decanting a rouged middle-aged blonde woman in a skintight, shimmering dress apparently constructed of iron filings, with an evening bag of the same material though in gold rather than silver, and a fake leopardskin wrap. Hooker, she looked like. She tripped across the rain-bouncing pavement in her gilt dancing pumps into the refuge of the doorway. Flashing a lipsticky smile at Alex she pressed the buzzer. A crackling male voice on the Ansaphone asked who was there. 'Georgina, darling. I'm alone.' She was buzzed in, and with another lipstick smile at Alex she opened the heavy door to negotiate, with some difficulty given the tightness of her dress, a steep flight of stairs. Everything in this town was either downstairs or upstairs. Didn't they have anything at ground level?

As the rain continued to bucket down there appeared, as through one of those glass-bead curtains to be found in Indian restaurants, the presence of Len Gates under a dripping golf umbrella, accompanied by a small cluster of Japanese tourists, each of them sheathed in identical transparent Pac-a-mac raincoats. 'Now, ladies and gentlemen, if you could but see in all this rain, the plaque on the wall here commemorates the fact that we are on the site of a burial pit for the Great Plague of 1665. Now it's said that, on occasion, shrouded figures . . .'

Len and his little party passed out of earshot as Alex's mobile trilled, the first call he'd had since coming south. Selby?

'Hello?'

'Ali? You were calling me.' Selby's mate Vicky. Must've gorrim on a 1471.

'Ah, right. Been clubbing, have we?'

'If you can call it that. Pineapple Grove. Dead. On top of which I have a row with Simon, wally that he is, right, and got back totally arsed, so if it's social chit-chat you're looking for, Ali, you've come to the wrong shop, right?'

'You know what I've been ringing you about, Vic. Have you spoken to her?'

'Since you ask. She called me from work, about fourish.'

'Work, what work?'

'The place that she's working at,' responded Vicky's voice carefully.

'Working at what?'

'Working at what she works at. Look, Ali, I'm very sorry, but let's get this over with, she doesn't want to see you, all right?'

'Did she say so? In so many words?'

'Not in so many words, no, but I've known Selby a long time, and if switching off her mobile isn't a hint, what is? She just wants to strike out on her own.'

'Strike out who with?' asked Alex jealously.

'There's nobody else, if that's what you mean, Ali, at least no one she's told me about.'

'So where will she be now?'

'In bed, I should think, at this time of night.'

Yeh yeh, in bed who with?

'In bed where?'

'Ali, leave it! Where are you speaking from, anyway?'

'So-oh.'

'Yes, well, she's nowhere near Soho for a start, I can

tell you that for nothing. I'm going to ring off now, Ali. I need my beauty sleep and I've got problems of my own.'

'With that Simon you're knocking around with? What's he been doing?'

'Too possessive, like someone else I could name but won't.'

'Meaning me?'

'You said it, Ali, I didn't. Night.'

Shit.

Not a bad looker, Vicky. Bit of a raver on the quiet, so he'd heard. Now that she was available, he'd have to keep her in mind. He didn't think she liked him, so that could be a problem, but it was one he could work on.

Meanwhile, it was beginning to sound like thank you and good night, Selby. So what now? The idea of the night coach to Leeds no longer appealed. What would it cost, anyway? What Alex had a need for was to get rat-arsed. Find this Gerry's Club, go back on the piss with James Flood, get monumentally arseholed, kip down somewhere, grabber bitter breakfast, then back to South Higginshaw in Dave's rhubarb truck.

That was if it ever stopped raining. It had never occurred to him to bring a raincoat at the beginning of May, in fact he never wore one. If it rained in Leeds you got pissed on, and that was that.

Possessive, eh? So what was wrong with being possessive? Better than treating them like shite. Though summer them seemed to go for it. Might be an idea to change his approach, trying it out on Vicky.

As he brooded on along these lines, and the downpour continued, one of Soho's cycle rickshaws splashed to the kerb and an attractive young woman climbed out and hurried into the doorway, vigorously shaking a stream of water from her umbrella. Familiar face. It was her, wasn't it? The lass in green. Christine, as she was called. Except that she wasn't wearing green now, she was dolled up to the nines in a backless electric blue satin number and ear-rings you could have started a hoop-la stall with.

'Nice weather for ducks,' said Alex pleasantly, but, in keeping with his new treat-'em-mean policy, unsmilingly.

'It's your original turn of phrase I like,' said Christine in a bantering way. 'Don't I know you from somewhere?'

'Yeh yeh, I grabbed your elbow in the street this evening. Mistook you for a friender mine.'

'So you did. You said you thought I was someone else, and I said, "Yes, I am," but you didn't get it.'

'Still don't,' confessed Alex. They could be talking Hindustani half the time down here, for all the sense you could get out of them. 'I'll tell you what, though. It's blurry wet out here – if that's a club down there, any chance of getting in?'

'Be my guest,' said Christine in her intriguingly deep voice.

Pressing the buzzer she spoke in response to the crackle from the other end: 'Christine, my love. I have someone with me, is that all right? No, he's straight. Or I think he is.'

What was that supposed to mean, then? There was something odd about this club. Worth having a dekko at, though. Good story for the lads, could be.

As they were buzzed through the stout door, Christine treated Alex to a winning smile. 'When I say be my guest, I should explain that there's a twenty-pound entry fee. But for that you get your first drink free.'

'Oh, well, that's all right, then, most reasonable.' But Alex's heavy sarcasm was lost on Christine. Fuming at having fallen for the trick like a mug tourist, he followed her down to a small lobby where he learned from the muscular woman guarding the door that by twenty pounds, Christine meant twenty pounds each, and that he was expected as a gentleman to pay her share. Another forty soddin quid down the drain. But too late to turn back now, Alex lad, without looking a complete wankah. As he paid up he saw with alarm that apart from loose change and a couple of fivers he was down to his last two twenty-pound notes.

Back on the beero, then. If Christine thought he was about to be pouring shampoo down her throat all night, she had another think coming. Christ, the money he'd got through, you would believe he had holes in his pockets. And if he happened to bump into Stephan Dance while he was getting through the rest of it, tough titty. What could he do? Alex swallowed hard. Chop his bollox off, that's what.

Blanking the thought out of his mind he tagged after Christine as she shimmied into what seemed to be a miniature dance hall, its once-varnished floor ringed by gilt-painted cane chairs obviously brought in by the van-load from some defunct *palais de danse*. Kinder stuff you saw in summer the crappier clubs of Leeds. Behind them the wallpaper was of the red flock variety still to be found in the Indian restaurants within chucking-up distance of the Metro.

But what intrigued Alex more than the décor was the clientele. Apart from a couple of bejeaned, bomber-jacketed blokes with gayish-looking droopy moustaches, and a like-wise bejeaned and T-shirted young girl with a battered beer tray who was waitressing for at a guess two pounds an hour, and looked to Alex a right little goer, the dozen or so inhabitants of the room were all flashily dressed women in their thirties to fifties. Two of them were dancing with each other to a tape of some twenties or thirties wah-wah stuff foreign to Alex. He recognised the one in the metallic sheath dress who had come down ahead of Christine, and he thought he knew the other one too from somewhere but couldn't place her. Tarty-looking brass-blonde, middle-aged, long grey flannel skirt, white frilly blouse.

And cross eyes.

Christ on crutches, it couldn't be. Oh, let it be, please. Even if it wasn't he would tell the lads it was, it was so priceless. And it was. The unembarrassed, cross-dressing squint-eyed waiter leered at Alex – or it could have been at Christine, it was difficult to say – as he foxtrotted by.

Odd how waiters were so difficult to place when you saw them out of uniform, he mused. Hey, that was funny! When he came to recount his adventures to the lads, he'd work it in.

Time to chat Christine up a bit, remembering to play it surly, not sound so eager. 'So is this a regular haunt of yours, then?'

'Only once a week. It gets expensive otherwise.'

Cheeky cat. It wasn't her forty quid he'd had to fork out. As for the free drink, the plastic tumblers the girl was taking round he could see contained the pissiest catpiss so far, and he hadn't even tasted his yet.

'You can say that again,' he said ruefully.

Christine touched his hand. 'Never mind, love, we'll see if we can make it worthwhile. Would you like to dance?'

He would, yes. Would like to feel her soft bod pressing up against his. But he couldn't do the foxtrot or the quick-step or the fookin rumba or whatever it was – the kinder dancing Alex did when he went clubbing, you made it up as you went along.

'Sorry, not my style,' he said gruffly.

'Is smiling your style?' asked Christine, smiling herself.

'What's that?' prompted Alex, who had been making rather a point of not smiling. Glad she'd noticed.

'I say you don't smile much, do you?'

'Not a lot, no.'

'Why – have you got bad teeth?'

She'd find that out soon as he got his tongue down her throat, he reckoned. He was wondering whether it was too early yet to verbalise this thought when one of the two or three young men in jeans and bomber jackets sashayed over. 'Good evening, Christine, and how's Christine? Haven't seen you in Madame Jo-Jo's lately.'

'That's because no one's invited me,' pouted Christine. The man half bowed to Alex. 'Do you mind if I ask Christine to dance? We're old friends.'

'Go ahead,' said Alex grudgingly. Actually he did mind, but since the bloke seemed to be gay he supposed no harm would come of it.

As the pair waltzed off around the tiny floor, if waltzing was what they were doing, he sipped cautiously from his plastic tumbler and took further stock of his surroundings.

On the other side of the dance floor, a youngish woman with long jet-black hair and, for this place, dressed rather quietly in a short corduroy skirt and white polo-necked jumper, was discreetly edging her way round towards the exit. Not so much edging, it seemed to Alex, as sidling. She stopped to clutch an errant ear-ring that was coming loose from its moorings, whereupon her eyes met, and locked with, Alex's.

Oh, Christ. They were pleading. As eloquently as if they could speak aloud, the heavily mascara-daubed eyes were saying: 'Please, Alex. Not a fookin word about this in South Higginshaw. Nobody up there knows and it'd kill me mam. And if word gets out at Butterfield's Rhubarb Farms I'm done for. Please, kidder, I'm begging you.'

Having transmitted this visual SOS, Dave slunk out with long, ungainly strides unbecoming in his tight skirt and high heels. Stroll on. This really was one for the lads. It would be all right – nonner them knew Dave, so he wouldn't be landing the poor bastard in the proverbial. And of course he would keep his gob shut over in South Higginshaw. After all, there were tales about Alex down in So-oh that Dave could spread, if he did but only know it.

No wonder he'd wanted Alex to keep out of Soho, though. Bang went that lift home. Dave would be too embarrassed to pick him up, for sure, and even if he did, Alex would be too embarrassed to sit next to him in the cab for two hundred miles. Buggeration. It was the coach, then, in the unlikely event of his having any money left. Or find his way to Nine Elms, New Covent Garden or whatever it was called, and cadge a lift from someone. There was bound to be a driver going north. Yeh yeh – fookin Dave. Oh, shite.

Alex let his gaze wander slowly around the room. The penny was dropping at last. He'd never been in a drag club before. Yeh yeh yeh yeh, they had one in Leeds, down by the canal, but he'd never been in it, and to the best of his knowledge he'd never met a cross-dresser. Till now. It was the square jawlines that were the giveaway, the only giveaway, in fact, because the way they were dolled up

– they must have taken hours getting ready – you could never have told they were all blokes, even, now he looked at her, the dishy little waitress. Blokes, every wunner them. All but the two or three men in bomber jackets. Well, the men were blokes too, obviously, but they weren't trying to pass themselves off as women.

And, in Christine's case at least, succeeding, for as the bloke who really was a bloke escorted her from the dance floor to rejoin him, it was difficult to take it in that Christine was a bloke too. Square jawline. Otherwise she was a dead ringer for a lass. How stupid of him. This one was definitely not for the lads.

'I hadn't realised this was a drag club,' said Alex with grotesque over-casualness as Christine sat down.

'It's been known for some people to spend the whole evening here without realising,' said Christine carelessly. 'Especially if Petra isn't in.'

'Who's Petra?'

Christine nodded towards the squint-eyed waiter in his white frilly blouse and chaste grey skirt, who by now had resumed his seat and was presumably gossiping to his former dancing partner, although apparently in conversation with an empty chair.

'Of course,' added Christine, 'they find out sooner or later if they get to take one of the girls home.'

'Why, what happens then?' Alex felt emboldened to ask. He was disturbed to discover from the faint stirring in his loins that this line of enquiry rather thrilled him.

'I don't know, you'd have to ask them,' said Christine archly.

Not that he would want any of this getting back to Leeds but it was strange how comfortable he still felt with Christine.

'So what's your real name, Christine?' he asked easily and this time without forcing it.

'My real name's Christine.'

'But you have another name, don't you? I mean what do your folks call you?'

'My folks? They don't know me.'

'All right, then, people at work, what name do you answer to when you're wearing a suit? Christopher?' he hazarded, correctly.

Or not correctly. 'Yes, but that's not me, can't you see that?'

Yeh yeh, he could see that, and he felt a sudden pang of – what was it? Sympathy? Pity? No, it wasn't, it was lust plain and simple.

Well, starting with Jenny Wise, and then moving on to the bizarre world of Brendan Barton, and now all this, no one could say he wasn't going right through the fookin card. Might as well, though. Blame Selby. And after that, forget it. Put it all down to a bad dream. Or a good one. Call it his kinky half-hour.

'I can see that, yes, Christine,' he said heavily, 'but what I'm a bit puzzled about is – well, come to the point, just what is it that you get out of this dressing-up malarkey?'

'I think what you mean, my love, is what you are likely to get out of it?'

Perceptive little thing, wasn't she? He? It? All right, yes. He'd no idea what was in store once they got back to Christine's place, which was where they would presumably end up. Who did what and to whom? The mind boggled. But whatever it was, he was up for it. You only lived once.

Yeh yeh yeh, and then you died of blurry Aids. Get out of it while you can, Alex lad.

No need. Taking his hand and patting it soothingly as she spoke, Christine said: 'I wish.'

'Come again?'

'Wishing's what it's all about, pet.'

'You mean you wish you were a woman?'

'I am a woman. But sometimes, owing to the quirks of nature, in men's clothes.'

She'd lost Alex. What was she saying – that she'd had the operation? 'I don't understand.'

'We're world-famous for not being understood, David.' He'd told her that was his name, in the belief that hers was Christine. Had he known there was another Dave on the premises when he came down here, he would have selected another.

'Let me tell you what you're trying to ask, and then I'll see if I can give you the answer.' He still found Christine's – Christopher's? – husky voice attractive, even though he now knew she was a bloke. If she still was a bloke, that was to say. Alex's knowledge of the anatomical ins and outs of sex-change were vague to non-existent. 'What you want to know is how I get my kicks, so's you'll know how you're going to get your kicks if and when the time comes.'

'Something like that, yeh yeh,' said Alex in a shamed voice.

'I can't speak for anyone else down here, but what I get out of this dressing-up malarkey, as you so charmingly put it, is that when a fanciable young man like you comes along and obviously finds me attractive, that's very gratifying. And that's how I get my satisfaction.'

'You mean you, er—?' Blushing again. He couldn't say it.

'Come?' Christine supplied the word. 'No, not that kind of satisfaction, pet, we can get all that at home. I mean mental satisfaction. You're a conquest, don't you know that?'

Yeh yeh yeh yeh. He hazily knew what Christine was on about. He'd known cock-teasers like this one.

But he plodded on, for he was beginning to suspect that it was cut-your-losses time.

'Very pleased to hear it, but I'm a bit hazy about these things, Christine. When you speak of getting all that at home, where do I fit into it exactly?'

'I'm afraid you don't, David,' said Christine, not without sadness. 'This is one of those cases where it only takes one to tango.'

So thank you and good night, Christine. Forty smackeroos down the pan. Pity. Still, between meeting Christine and not having met Christine, he was glad he had chosen the former course.

7

Gerry's Club, when it was finally located for him at the foot of Dean Street by a drunk who wanted to go in with him but whom he had the intelligence to shake off, was everything that Alex Singer required of So-oh.

It was babbling with noise and at two in the morning bubbling with people. A shit-hot jazz pianist in a spade hat benignly told him, after he had fought through the room to request 'When The Saints Go Marching in', that he would sooner play the failed Icelandic entry for the Eurovision Song Contest. Every second person was a celeb, major to minor. It was like the Christmas number of the fookin *Radio Times*. Sitcom stars. Soap actors. Wunner the cast of that new film release, what was it called?, got a good mensh in *What's On In Leeds*. That black guy outer that soccer-quiz prog. That DJ with the teeth. Jesus.

But because James Flood had drilled it into him three times over before departing for the Groucho, he knew enough not to speak to any of them unless he was spoken to and definitely not to ask for autographs. Didn't mind that at all. It was cool, in fact, mingling with this lot and pretending he rubbed shoulders with this classer personality every nighter the week.

One person, though, was entitled to his attention, or rather, he was entitled to hers. Jenny Wise was perched at the very end of the bar, the preferred position, as Alex was beginning to realise, for women of, how should he put this, an adventurous disposition. She was alone and, sipping coffee, seemed sober again. Remarkable. Alex could no longer remember where he had last seen her during this long night, or what condition she'd been in, but she was evidently one of those women – not that he had previously encountered many, or indeed any, of the breed – who when it came to alcoholic damage were perpetually self-healing, like what the fook was that mythological beast that crawled out of the flames unscathed? Or grew another head was it? At this timer night he couldn't remember which. Anyway, that.

No sign of James Flood. Alex edged his way back through the thronged little room – why couldn't they make these Soho joints bigger, to accommodate the demand? – until he was alongside Jenny.

'How you doing, Jen?' he asked cockily. He could be well in here, it seemed to Alex. Quick shag back at her place then a kip down for the night. Sorted. No chance of breakfast, he supposed, Jenny being Jenny, but even so it was still two birds with one stone.

'Who the fuck are you, darling?' asked Jenny evenly, with an offputting stare.

Not so sober after all. But Jesus Christ almighty, did they all suffer from collective blurry amnesia in So-oh? It was only – well, he didn't know how many hours, but it wasn't all that long ago since he'd got his leg across with Jenny, and she didn't know him from fookin Adam.

'We have met,' he said helpfully, adding with a wealth of meaning: 'Round at your place.'

'When was that, darling?'

'Earlier today. We went on from the New Kismet Club.'

'Everything's on from the New Kismet. Narrow it down.'

'You said you liked my accent.' In point of fact she'd said it was cute, but he didn't want to bring that up again.

'Oh, right. You were from Lancashire.'

'Yorkshire.'

'Same thing. Don't tell me, don't tell me – it's Adam, isn't it?'

'Alex.' Or had he been calling himself Adam? It was so long ago he couldn't remember. But since she couldn't either, it made no difference. 'Would you like a drink?'

'They won't serve you, honey. Not a member. Besides, the Old Bill's in.'

'I meant round at your place, if there's any of that Scotch left.'

'What Scotch is that, Alan?'

'What we were drinking earlier.'

'When was that?'

Alex decided on the big bold approach. 'Look, Jenny. We had a good time a few hours ago. Or at least I thought we did. Why don't we go back and have a good time again?'

''S time?' slurred Jenny.

'Just after two.'

'Sorry, honeybunch,' said Jenny, not without regret. 'You were yesterday. I'm looking for tomorrow.'

And bollox to you too, Jen-Jen. She picked up her cup of coffee and moved away, either to talk to a friend or make a new one. The guvnor of the club, as James assumed him to be, a grey-haired, distinguished, bearded type who looked as if he could have made a living posing for the Player's cigarette packet, came into the bar from the tiny kitchen. He'd evidently been asked to look out for Alex. 'Your friend James is over there,' he said. 'He needs cheering up.'

Not the only one, thought Alex, feeling unaccountably depressed after his exchange with Jenny.

He found James Flood at a corner table sharing a bottle of wine with a youngish, dark-suited man of athletic build who could have been either a footballer or a copper. He would prove to be the latter.

He was introduced to Alex as Benny Wills. 'And what do you do, Benny?' asked Alex chattily. After a few hours in London, the social graces were coming more easily.

Wills glanced a query at James, who nodded reassurance and supplied the information: 'Detective inspector, Clubs and Vice Squad.'

Yeh yeh yeh yeh, heard of it. Read about it in the *News of the Screws*. Opportunity for a wisecrack here: 'Well, Benny, we've found the clubs, but where's the vice?'

'One hundred and forty-five,' said Detective Inspector Wills, deadpan.

'Wossat, then?'

'Number of times he's heard that joke,' explained James.

'Tonight,' added the detective, glumly.

Lead balloon time. Change subject. 'How did you get on at the Groucho, James?'

'Pissed on from a great height,' said James.

'Yeh yeh, I got caught in it too.'

'I'm not talking about the rain, I'm talking about my stupid pissballing editor. I've given that fucking paper three stories today and what did she say?'

'I dunno, what did she say?'

'Chewed my bollox off. Said I wasn't paid to sit around in Soho clubs getting pissed all day.'

'I thought you were. Sounded just the job to me.'

'If it is, there's about to be a vacancy. If I don't get something in tomorrow's paper, that's it. *Finito*.'

'Well, I suppose there's other papers,' said Alex vaguely. Didn't claim to know much about these things.

'Not when you've been thrown off the *Examiner*, there aren't,' said Detective Inspector Wills. Then, glancing towards the stairs, he added to James Flood: 'Here's a bit of a tale for you, Jas.'

James looked up to see the two flymen coming down into the club, but without the burden of their lately departed friend. The jazz pianist obligingly played a snatch of the Dead March from *Saul* as they reached the bar. 'I was with them earlier,' he said. 'She's not interested. Wouldn't know a human story if it came up and bit her in the crotch.'

'How earlier is earlier? You know they were nicked tonight, don't you?'

'For what?' asked James Flood, livelier now.

'Good question. Last I heard when I checked in, the duty desk sarge was trying to frame a charge for them.'

'Frame being the operative word, eh, Benny?'

'Watch it, James,' advised the policeman, without rancour.

The two flymen, clutching a bottle of beer each, shoved their way through the throng to James's table. Addressing Detective Inspector Wills, the first flyman said: 'Tell you what, Benny. That canteen bacon you dish up at that nick of yours is pigshit.'

'Right animal, anyway,' said Detective Inspector Wills. 'Don't blame me, it's all done by a private catering firm since you were last banged up. So what are you doing out, then?'

'Police bail,' said the second flyman. 'All the cells are taken. We're up at Marlborough Street tomorrow.'

'What charge?'

'Obstruction. And sunnink to do with the London Transport laws.'

'Taking a dead body on the tube?' said James. 'I didn't know that was illegal.'

'It is if he didn't have a ticket,' the detective inspector pointed out.

'But he did have a ticket,' protested the first flyman. 'He had his old people's travel pass, didn't he?'

'Ah, but it's invalid if he's dead,' said Detective Inspector Wills. 'The conditions of carriage clearly state that when the pass expires, or in this case the passholder expires, it has to be handed in.'

'How could he hand it in when he's flaming dead?' demanded the exasperated second flyman.

'I dunno, mate. He should've thought of that before he kicked the bucket.'

'What have you done with Old Jakie, anyway?' asked Alex. Another for the lads, this.

'They confiscated him,' explained the first flyman. 'He got stuck as we were getting him through the ticket barrier. They had to call the fire brigade to cut him free. Then they handed him over to the wossname, council environmental health service, poor sod.'

'So how come it's us that's charged with obstruction?' asked the aggrieved second flyman of the detective. 'It was Old Jakie causing the flaming obstruction, not us.'

'You were aiding and abetting,' said Detective Inspector Wills solemnly. 'Comes to the same thing. The beak might take the view that it's even worse. You were inciting him to commit an offence.'

'So what do you reckon we'll get?'

With a broad wink at James and Alex, the detective

inspecter said: 'Could be six months, could be two years if the Stipe's in a bad mood.'

'You're pulling our pissers!' said the second flyman uncertainly.

'On the other hand, if he's in a good mood, you might just get away with a twenty-quid fine.'

With a sigh of relief the first flyman said: 'Worth every penny, for the sake of giving him a last night out at the Shamrock Club up Camden Town. Only it's a good thing he didn't get stuck in the ticket barrier going out instead of coming back, cos he really enjoyed himself up there.'

'Seemed to,' said the second flyman. 'I'll swear there was a smile on his face when we bought him that last pint of Guinness.'

'What did you do with it?' asked James Flood, with a journalist's curiosity.

'Oh, opened his gob and poured it down his throat. You'd've thought with all he'd got down him in one place or another it would've come up again, but it didn't. Mebbe it did later, over the social workers. With any luck.'

Cackling, the two flymen drifted away to greet friends. Alex noted jealously that they seemed to be best mates with half the telly stars in London. And them only blurry scene-shifters. You couldn't say it wasn't democratic down here.

The shit-hot jazz pianist in the spade hat broke off from his rendering of 'Smoke Gets In Your Eyes' to interpolate a snatch of silent cinema chase music as a wild-eyed Kim Grizzard came charging down the stairs. It seemed to be the pianist's policy to introduce selected club members with their own theme tune.

Grizzard, having spotted James Flood's corner table from the half-landing, barged his way through to it.

'He's not here,' supplied James hastily.

'And if he was,' said Detective Inspector Wills, 'I should have to take you in for – lemme see, what do you want to do to him, assault and battery or GBH?'

'It'll be murder when I catch the bastard,' snarled Grizzard.

'Well, you certainly won't find him down here, because he's barred. He'll be in bed at this hour I should imagine, stoned out of his brains.'

'No, he isn't, I've just been round to his place and kicked the door in, and he's not there.'

'Shouldn't've told me that, Kim,' tut-tutted the policeman, with another owlish wink at James. 'Breaking and entering, malicious damage, you name it.'

'He won't lodge a complaint, Benny, because he knows what he'd get if he did. Anyway,' and here Kim Grizzard fixed a baleful eye upon Alex, who had been hunched up in his chair, doing his best to look inconspicuous, 'as it happens it's not him I'm after at this immediate moment in time. All right, you, where is it?'

'Where's what?' piped up Alex in the high-pitched voice that seemed to visit him in moments of stress.

'The manuscript of *Freeze When You Say That*. The only bastardising copy.'

'I haven't got it,' confessed Alex. With a policeman present he felt on reasonably safe ground for the time being.

'Then you're in deep shit, man. I left that script with you for safe-keeping.'

'I didn't ask for your blurry script – it's nowt to do wi' me!' Not only did Alex's voice rise in times of stress, it slipped into the broadest West Yorkshire, the accent he had grown up with.

'Tell him, Benny,' sighed Grizzard, full of despair and weariness.

'Civil matter,' adjudicated Detective Inspector Wills.

'All right, so it's a civil matter. Tell him he's going to have to sell his house.'

'I don't have a house,' volunteered Alex.

'Then you'd better fucking buy one, because if that script doesn't turn up you are in double doo-doo, my friend. Now where do you think you lost it?'

'I haven't lost it, I've just left it somewhere,' Alex thought he'd better say.

'All right, where do you think you left it?'

'I can tell you where I didn't leave it,' said Alex helpfully. 'And that's that Kemble's Club, because that's where I noticed it were missing. But I definitely had it when we left that Eyetie restaurant, Baldini's is it?'

Here Detective Inspector Wills took charge of the proceedings. Now sounding like the copper he was, he said: 'If you're sure you had it when you left, it don't matter a fuck whether it was Baldini's or Burger King. Now where were you between Baldini's and Kemble's Club?'

'A lorrer pubs. He'll know better than me.' Alex inclined his head towards James, who had nodded off.

Snapping out of a light doze upon the question being repeated, James recited: 'Coach, French, Pillars of Hercules, Blue Posts, Three Greyhounds, Admiral Duncan, Wellington Arms.'

'Fuck me,' said the detective. 'I'm not surprised he lost the bloody script. With that itinerary, I'm only amazed you both made it down here with your heads intact.'

'My usual beat,' said James Flood modestly.

'No wonder that tight-arsed editress of yours complains you never get any stories. You do get them, but they've gone clean out of your mind by the time you reach Kemble's.'

Kim Grizzard had been furiously scribbling down the list of pubs on a scrap of paper. To Alex: 'Now. Opening time tomorrow morning, you and I are going to do a tour of all these pubs.'

'Not me, mate,' said Alex, emboldened by the burly proximity of a policeman. 'I'll be on my way back up to Leeds by then. Important appointment.' At this hour, though, he couldn't remember what it was.

'You'll be on your way back to nowhere, my friend. You have even more important appointments with the Coach and Horses, the French House—'

'Leave it, Kim,' soothed the detective inspector. 'You can't make him stay if he don't want to. Habeas fucking corpus. Anyway, between the two of you, you'd get so pissed you'd forget what you was looking for.'

'Six months out of my life, that's what we'll be looking for!' Kim Grizzard favoured Alex with another glower. 'All right, get back to bloody Lancashire or wherever you come from, but I shall want your address.'

'Leeds Metropolitan University.'

'Your home address, prat.'

'You mean the house I've gotter sell?' asked Alex cheekily.

'Give it to him, laddie,' counselled Detective Inspector Wills. 'He's entitled.'

'We're talking hardback rights, paperback rights, American rights, foreign rights, film rights, video rights . . . If I don't get that script back you could well be paying out for it for the rest of your life.'

Not me, buster, thought Alex. We're talking about me emigrating to Australia, sharpish, if need be. But he wasn't going to lose sleep over it. It was just the way they banged on down here. Larger than life, that was the expression.

'What's this book of yours called again?' asked James, looking the picture of innocence as he tapped Alex on the ankle, at the same time winking at the detective inspector, a practice they seemed to go in for with their peculiar sense of humour.

'*Freeze When You Say That*, why?'

'It's just that I thought I heard Ellis Hugo Bell mention a novel of that title.'

'Can't have done, I've never even mentioned it to him after the sod pissed me about over the last one. And then, as we now know, nicked the plot.'

'He could have read it by now, though, couldn't he?' said Detective Inspector Wills seriously, joining in James's legpull.

Wild-eyed again, Grizzard stared in turn at the detective, at the reporter, and at the visiting Yorkshireman. He then bounded to his feet, gulped down the remainder of Alex's wine, and leaped up the stairs, accompanied by appropriate silent cinema music from the shit-hot jazz pianist in the spade hat who, with Grizzard's exit safely effected, reverted to the Scott Joplin number he had been strumming.

Alex, more out of nervousness than appreciation of the music, began compulsively tapping his foot, although on the offbeat, knowing nothing about jazz except that he knew what he liked, and it wasn't that fookin modern stuff.

He was also, to a completely different beat, drumming a hand on the table while jerking his head in and out like an agitated terrapin. An embarrassed James Flood, avoiding the musician's amused eye across the room, said: 'If you like jazz, Alex, why don't we go down the Blue Note?'

'What, at this blurry hour? Will they still be open?'

'They won't even have started yet,' said Detective Inspector Wills. 'They go down there to jam among themselves, after doing a few sets at Ronnie Scott's and wherever.'

Suited Alex. The longer he fought off sleep the less of a problem it was going to be to find somewhere to lay down his head for what remained of the night. Someone had told him there was a twenty-four-hour McDonald's in Leicester Square, wherever that might be. Must be near that tube station of the same name that he'd got out at after he'd been dropped at King's Cross by Dave, seemed weeks ago now. Black coffee, McMuffin, and a few sly zeds before dawn broke or he got chucked out, whichever came the sooner. Then sod it, sod Selby, sod the lorrer them, he was off. Get back somehow, he'd think about it in the morning.

'You coming down, Benny?' asked James ingratiatingly, the reporter sucking up to the law.

'Nah,' the policeman said. 'I was in last night. I want to look in at that new lesbo club in Rupert Street.'

'Thought it had been closed down for having no licence?'

'It has. I want to check if it's still open. Might see you for a nightcap afterwards, down the Waiters Club.'

Nightcap? Fookin hell. Didn't these people have homes to go to?

'All right, Benny, seeya layer.'

'Seeya layer.'

As Alex rose, echoing, 'Seeya layer,' in a worldly way,

he saw Jenny Wise threading her way through the room, clutching, as if he were a fairground prize, the hand of a young, handsome and currently rather sheepish-looking actor he recognised from one of the soaps.

As they climbed the stairs, the shit-hot jazz pianist in the spade hat played Jenny a little exit music. 'Tomorrow', from the musical *Annie*.

Now Alex understood why he'd been played off with the Beatles' 'Yesterday' when he detached himself from Jenny after her brush-off at the bar.

8

So this Barry Chilton was a poet, was he, so what? Alex had met poets before, in fact Leeds was overrun with the buggers. Pub he used to go to, the Frog and Firkin, used to have Monday night poetry readings before they changed the policy and turned it into a Quiz Nite. The poems were mainly by students like himself and he didn't much reckon them, they were like the ones you used to write at school, wind blowing, leaves swirling, all that kinder shite. He supposed this bugger's would be the same.

Say this for him, though. First time he'd ever known a poet buy a blurry drink. Probably just sucking up to James Flood, wanted to get his name in the *Examiner*.

And this was the famous Blue Note, was it? The usual crummy basement. If the Thames came up from wherever it was and So-oh got fookin flooded, the whole district would go bankrupt. Or their insurance companies would; but moster them didn't look insured to Alex, admittedly no expert in these matters. Coupler dozen punters mebbe, sitting at what looked like old kitchen tables, with candles stuck in wine bottles providing the only illumination. Sprinkling of black guys, they looked like proper jazz buffs. Strong smell of spliffs, Alex wondered what Detective Inspector Wills had made of it when he was in last night. Usual catpiss wine. Over there sat Jenny Wise with that young bloke from the TV soap. Alex wondered if he'd scored yet. Or, perhaps more to the point, if she had.

The set had not yet begun. The saxophonist and the clarinet player, both of them ageing with grey sixties sideboards, unpacked their instruments and began tuning up. While the generous Barry Chilton bought a bottle of wine at the serving hatch that doubled as cloakroom and box office, Alex mused on events since leaving Gerry's Club.

It had continued to be a curious evening. Curious morning rather, by this time. Falling out of Gerry's Club Alex was surprised to find Dean Street, at three a.m., as lively, livelier in fact, as it had been twelve hours ago. Few places were open now – itinerant hot-dog sellers, their aluminium carts portable and powerful stench-carriers, had moved in to fill the market gap created by the closed cafés and restaurants. What the punters were doing now was promenading, sauntering about and breathing in the warm air, fresh after the summer rain. Either that or waiting for the taxis that never came. There were touts on the street: mini-cab touts, drug touts, near-beer club touts, hotel touts, pimps, as James knowledgeably identified them. It was a working street still: everybody had an angle.

They turned into Old Compton Street, to the corner where he'd started his long Soho odyssey so many hours, or was it days, ago. The scene was much the same as earlier, except that the shops and bars were closed and most of their doorways were occupied by the blanket-shrouded homeless. From the kitchens of the closed-down restaurants, ruffianly looking commis chefs and washers-up were emerging blinking into the half-dawn, like rats ascending from the sewers, before hurrying off, so James said, to lose their night's earnings in the Chinese gambling clubs around Gerrard Street. A beggar asked for change.

Following James's lead, Alex ignored him. Giving hand-outs was not cool.

As they passed the narrow entry to Compton's Yard, the home of Kemble's Club, they heard a familiar sing-song voice: '. . . And in this humble little alley, ladies and gentlemen, was situated, until he was embraced by fame, the engraving shop of William Hogarth, renowned for his portrayals of London life such as *The Rake's Progress*. This very yard, it has been suggested, may have been the inspiration for his Gin Alley . . .'

'His late late show,' explained James. 'They come in on the long-haul red-eye, sleep all the way over then can't sleep when they get here. He rounds them up in the hotel lobbies.'

Alex abruptly interrupted this dissertation: 'Can you smell burning?'

'Chip-pan fire,' said James Flood, sniffing the air.

'Bollox. Nobody's cooking chips at this timer night, not even in So-oh.'

Led by a tired-looking Len Gates, who was now delivering an on-the-hoof droning monologue about how Soho had once been the main centre for tapestry manufacture in the capital, and how Hogarth had taken one Joshua Morris, a craftsman, to the Court of Common Pleas for failing to pay for a tapestry he had commissioned, a crocodile of bleary-eyed Californians was shuffling out into Old Compton Street. In contra-flow to them, Alex and James drifted down into Compton's Yard and yes, there was definitely a smell of burning.

There was Kemble's Club, closed by now, and next to it a derelict building, possibly Hogarth's old workshop, boarded up, half gutted, awaiting work to be done on it to transform it into what? Restaurant? Club? Bar? Coffee shop? Any or all of these things. And next to that was, oh, fook, he hadn't noticed it the first time round – *Eve's Erotica. Adult video's – book's – mag's. Sale or rent. Poppers*. And if the shop wasn't on fire, what was that flickering glow, visible through a half-open door, in the back basement?

'Sod me, hadn't we better ring 999?'

'I shouldn't think that's necessary,' said James Flood uneasily.

'But it's a fire brigade job is this, Jas! The whole blurry place'll be going up in a minute!'

'You heard what your friend said, son. It won't be necessary. Put your mobile away.'

Stephan Dance, a light camelhair overcoat draped over his shoulders and clutching a set of car keys, stood behind them. To both Alex's and James's surprise, he was accompanied by Detective Inspector Wills of the Clubs and Vice Squad.

'Told you there was a smell of burning, Stephan,' said the detective. 'Good thing I bumped into you – a minute later and you'd have been vrooming off to Monk Wood St Mary's in that white Roller of yours, and come back tomorrow to a smouldering ruin.'

'It's only some rags and stuff in the back room, Benny. I'll soon have it out. My own fault for smoking down there.'

'Doing your VAT returns, were you?'

'Something like that. Paperwork.'

'So, if it's only rags and stuff, you won't need to bother the insurance company, will you?'

'Shouldn't think so, Benny, no.'

'Wouldn't want you to lose your no-claims bonus, would we? Well, you'd better get that fire extinguisher out, Stephan, before it takes hold. You'll be doing that, will you, Stephan?'

'On the case now, Benny, no probs. Seeya, Benny.'

'Seeya, Stephan.'

A petulant Stephan Dance let himself into the shop, where in a few moments he could be observed reluctantly sprinkling the blaze. Smiling inscrutably to himself, Detective Inspector Wills nodded to Alex and James and went on his way.

'If that wasn't blurry arson, I don't know what is,' muttered Alex as they too meandered out into Old Compton Street. 'Why didn't he nick the bugger?'

'Probably because the bugger's more use to the Old Bill out of Wormwood Scrubs than in it,' said James Flood with a sagacity beyond his years.

Cleansed by a brief flurry of rain, Old Compton Street was quieter now, so that the sight of six waiters wearing ankle-length, Aubrey Beardsley-type white aprons, and each carrying a tin tray laden with a bottle of champagne and two glasses as they hurried – ran, almost – along the middle of the street, was even more surreal than it might otherwise have been.

'Rehearsal for the annual Waiters' Race,' said James helpfully. 'They have to go up Greek Street, round Soho Square, down Frith Street, along Romilly Street and finish up outside Kettner's without spilling a drop.'

The rear of the peculiar procession was brought up by a plump, panting waiter who rattled metallically as he waddled along. A further explanation from the knowledgeable James: 'Soup spoons. That's the guy from Baldini's who starts at Pizza Heaven in the morning. If you remember, the spoons are his dowry.'

'So I'm not seeing things after all,' said Alex in

mock-relief. 'What with all the booze I've taken on board today and being on the go for Christ knows how many hours, I thought for a minute it were a fookin mirage.'

And so to the flickering candlelight of the Blue Note, where pianist, drummer and bass were now joining the saxophonist and clarinettist on the little stage as Barry Chilton threaded his way through the tables with a bottle of wine.

'So where yow from, kid?' asked the friendly poet as he sat down. 'Lydes? I've plyed a few gigs in Lydes.' Brummie, he was. Big bearded Brummie. Alex regarded him with some respect now that James had told him that, for a poet, Barry was quite famous. One of the Soho Poets, whoever they were. Been on *The Brendan Barton Show*, when Brendan Barton had a show to go on. Late-night BBC2 stuff. Did Sunday night gigs in pubs. But what he was best known for, it seemed, was a kind of English rap, which he did to a saxophone accompaniment. Alex wondered if he could persuade him to play the Metro studio theatre. Could be a feather in his cap, getting him up there. Best wait and see if he was any cop first, though.

A drumroll as the pianist, who doubled as MC, rose holding a stick microphone. 'Lydies and gentlemen.' He too had a strong Black Country twang. 'Welcome to the Blue Note, the club that put the zeds in jazz. The club that charges more to let you out than to let you in. Allow me to introduce our little group. You've heard of the Birmingham Six, this is the Birmingham Five. We're on trial here tonight. If they find us guilty we have to go back to Brum . . .'

The banter continued, each quip punctuated by a drum-beat. Barry Chilton murmured that the man had filched most of his material from Ronnie Scott's. Then after a few minutes the quintet began to play. It was stuff that was not familiar to Alex, bit modern it sounded, but they were good – not as good as the shit-hot pianist in the spade hat down in Gerry's Club but worth a listen.

After three or four numbers there was a break, during which Alex saw Jenny Wise and the young bloke from the soap sneaking out, jammy bugger that he was. He'd already had his arm up her skirt as far as his shoulder-blade, just about, while she'd been snogging him like a boa constrictor swallowing a rabbit, so it shouldn't take them all that long to consummate what they had commenced. If you asked Alex, they wouldn't get further than the nearest back alley.

The spectacle had not gone unnoticed by the pianist MC. Nor by the audience. 'Lydies and gentlemen, now you know why they call this club the Blue Room. There is no extra charge for the bed show.' Ribald applause. Alex wondered how Jenny Wise felt about putting herself up for this sort of thing, or whether she even knew. Nonner his business, but it was a bit sad, like.

'. . . Meanwhile, we have the sixth member of the Birmingham Five, the one that got away, it's dead easy to get away from Brum, lydies and gentlemen, you just stand at the side of the M1 with a sign that says "Anywhere". Tonight he's come all the way from the Coach and Horses to be with us, please welcome Mr Barry Chilton . . .'

Barry was already on his feet and bounding to the stage. All the musicians save the saxophone trooped off as he took the microphone and the saxophonist came forward and played a few random riffs.

His first short lyric was a skilfully extemporised and highly defamatory one about Jenny Wise and her young conquest, of which the only words Alex could remember later, to his regret, were 'He's got the class, she's got the ass.' Nor, when he came to a haunting rap ballad about unrequited love, backed by a muted saxophone accompaniment as melancholy as the klaxon of one of those American freight trains crossing the prairie you saw in old westerns, could Alex remember any of that either, except the line, 'She wouldn't say and she wouldn't stay.' Story of his life, that was.

It wasn't what he would have called a pome, more of a story, if a simple one. But it was blurry good. It told how this chick, not a cock-teaser because they were on shagging terms, nevertheless kept her bloke at arm's length, and whenever he tried to get near her mentally as well as physically was as elusive as a butterfly. At the end she left, she wouldn't say where but he didn't care, because she'd gone long before he'd found her. Something along those lines, anyway. Whether it was the poignant lyric or the poignant music that had the effect, Alex would have been hard put to say, but to his embarrassment a plump tear rolled down his cheek.

Maybe it was just the booze weeping. Maybe it was the hour – getting on for four by now, a notoriously suicidal time. But he had an urgent need to speak to Selby, hear her voice, even if she told him to piss off.

Would she have left her mobile on? Only one way to find out. It was a long shot, but there was just the possibility that she left it on in the small hours in case of emergency, like her dad having a blurry heart-attack or something. Worth a try, mood he found himself in.

He waited until Barry Chilton went into a huddle with the saxophonist about his next number, flashed his mobile at James to signal what he was doing, and darted up the stairs into the street.

He hadn't particularly noticed where he was going after they'd left Gerry's Club but he knew he was on one of those streets leading up from Shaftesbury Avenue – Dean, Frith, Greek; alphabetical order as James had taught him. It was very quiet now, the only sounds being distant, sporadic traffic, ambulance sirens and Barry Chilton's recitative voice from down in the Blue Note, backed by the plaintive saxophone. Couldn't make out the lyric but it was making them laugh; maybe he should have stayed down there and snapped out of his gloompot mood.

Greek Street, it seemed to be. A black guy stood on the corner under the street lamp, cigarette glowing – pusher most likely. Or not: if he were, he might as well wear a placard around his neck saying, 'Arrest me'. On the other side stood a white guy in a mac, waiting for a hooker. Or a cab, you couldn't tell which. He would get neither at this hour, if you asked Alex.

He stood in a wine shop doorway and punched out Selby's mobile number. No result. Shit. Didn't feel like returning to the Blue Note for a few minutes, he could do with a cup of black coffee if there was one going anywhere at coming up to four. McDonald's, Leicester Square, someone had said. How far away was that?

Idly, he crossed the street. There was an unlit little alley opposite, no more than an extended gap between the buildings of Greek Street, housing what looked like a block of run-down flats, knocking-shops he would guess, and a porn shop and bed show, very likely the property of Stephan Dance. Hog Court. Bit like Compton's Yard where he'd encountered Dance earlier. Narrow shave he must've had with that bugger. If Detective Inspector Wills had not been in attendance, a dark alley at four in the morning was not the place to meet a Soho pornographer who had undertaken to recover Brendan Barton's fifty pounds.

Alex shuddered. Whether it was the shudder or the dark inviting proximity of Hog Court that suddenly brought it on he couldn't say, but he had a pressing desire for a jimmy riddle. When had he last had one? Christ, it muster been hours ago, no wonder he was bursting for a leak. The Wellington Arms, was it? And there'd been wunner them Post-it slips stuck to the bog wall, with the message: 'Does anyone ever see Big John who used to come in here and Muriel's? He liked a drink and a fight.' Underneath, someone had scrawled: 'RIP.' Said it all about So-oh, that did.

As he edged furtively towards the little alley, conscious as always on these occasions that he was probably committing an offence by peeing in public, Alex all but bumped into the squint-eyed waiter, now back in mufti and wearing an ankle-length white apron and carrying a tray laden with champagne bottle and glasses. A lone rehearsal runner for the Waiters' Race, he zigzagged erratically backwards and forwards across Greek Street as he hurried towards Soho Square.

Out of the shadows of Hog Court there now emerged a figure who had clearly been engaged on a similar mission to Alex's. Dapper, middle-aged, clerkly-looking character carrying a neatly-folded raincoat. Alex thought he vaguely recognised him as he bustled off down Greek Street. Yes, seen the bugger before, where was it now? Wellington Arms, jimmy riddle, Post-it slip for whoever it was, Big John, and he'd come out of the bog and this sad sack was sitting at a table nursing half a Guinness and toying with a Swiss Army knife. As you do. So what was he doing wandering the streets at this God-forsaken hour?

Been shagging a hooker, probably. Or trying to, poor sod looked as if he couldn't get it up. Anyway, nonner his business.

Slipping into Hog Court, Alex was unzipping himself when he heard a rustling sound from some feet away. Oh, shite, who was it this time? Could be Jenny Wise and the randy young telly bloke having it away, too impatient to go round to her place. No, it was the rustle of a plastic raincoat as the lamplight from Greek Street fell on the frightened face of that old bat he'd given the book to. What was she called again? Else.

Didn't know him from Adam, of course. But she clutched his sleeve and whispered urgently: 'Young man, you must come with me!'

Dotty or what? And this was someone else who was out at all hours. Didn't she have a home to go to? Could be she didn't. And where was the fookin thirty-quid book he'd bought her? Left it in some pub lav, he shouldn't wonder.

He allowed Else to take his arm and steer him across the alley, chattering excitedly: 'I'd just come down here for a little wee-wee, because I suffer from a weak bladder, you know, I expect when you reach my age you'll have the same problem. And I was just doing what I had to do, when I noticed a man standing over that young lady there, lying on the ground. He saw me and hurried away and I came over as soon as I was able and looked at her. I thought at first she was drunk, because they do drink far too much nowadays, these gels, but now I'm not so sure, I think she may be dead.'

They had reached the body of Christine Yardley, a.k.a. Christopher, lying face downwards outside the door of her rickety block of flatlets next to the darkened bed show, and clutching a bunch of keys. She was still wearing the backless electric blue satin number he'd seen her in at the Transylvania Club, but it was pulled up nearly to her waist to reveal twisted, laddered stockings that looked pathetically tawdry in the half-light of dawn.

'Or she could well have been raped, although I see she's still wearing her knickers. Do you know how to give the kiss of life, young man?'

No, did he hell, but in any case she was so still she looked as if she'd already had the kiss of death. Crouching, Alex gingerly clutched Christine's still-warm shoulder and turned her over on to her side. The electric blue satin was black now with the blood that still bubbled through it from the slashing wound in her stomach. The blood that had trickled from her mouth and down her chin to the crevice of her neck where she had haemorrhaged glistened wetly. Her eyes were staring.

'Oh dear, do you think we should perhaps find a policeman?' twittered Else, nervously rubbing flaking skin from her hands.

Alex staggered to his feet, turned away, tottered a few shuffling steps and was copiously and noisily sick. There was tomato in it, as always.

9

It had been the last eventful hour of a long eventful day.
Or perhaps it was the first eventful hour of a new one,
who could say?

Whichever, Alex was shagged out. So, where was he
again? Right, the Waiters Club in Gerrard Street, because
it said so on the short, plastic-covered egg-and-chips menu
on the Formica tables. Did chefs and waiters go in for
egg and chips, then, he wondered irrelevantly. Must do.
They'd get pissed off with serving that fancy muck all
night and would want something plain when it was their
turn to eat. Be that as it may, how had he got to the
Waiters Club?

Presumably James and that Barry Chilton had brought
him here, carried him here for all he knew, because they
were both sitting opposite him, James scribbling furiously
on some scraps of wrapping paper he had cadged from
behind the bar. But he had no recollection of getting here.
Not because of being pissed, he'd stopped being pissed
when he'd thrown up, or so he told himself. No, it was
because of the shock. Trauma. Or so he told himself.

All right, Alex, think back, step by step. Christine's
body, belching blood. Batty old Else, wittering away like
a fookin sparrow. 'Do you think we'd better find a
policeman?' she'd said. We. Both of us. You and me. And
he'd left her to it, shit that he was. No wonder he'd
blanked it out of his memory.

No, no, it wasn't as bad as that, and after all, it was her corpse, she was the one who'd found it, there was nothing he could add, and look at it this way, he had to get back to Leeds. And if there hadn't been a police car cruising by he was sure he wouldn't have run out on her, not that he had run, he'd walked, briskly; but as it so happened there was indeed a police car, cruising along Old Compton Street, so he saw no harm in leaving her with the Old Bill. Should've given her his name, he supposed, but the silly old cow would never have remembered it, and anyway, what for? She had the full story, or as full a story as anybody had at this stage.

So he left her waving down the patrol car and, there was no other word for it, slunk off, following the siren sound of a jazz quintet that was floating on the early-morning breeze, and presently finding himself back in the sanctuary of the Blue Note.

'So yow left poor old Else to it?' said Barry Chilton brutally, when he and James had heard about his adventure.

'Why not? It's her story, let her have the glory,' said Alex defensively.

'It's not her story, it's my story,' said James Flood, glancing at his watch and knocking back his wine. 'Come on, let's go.'

But it took some time to get the bill, or rather for Alex to get the bill, since it appeared to be his shout for the second bottle that had been plonked down during Barry Chilton's set, so that by the time they got across to Hog Court it was already swarming with police officers, who were stretching black and yellow tape across the alley even as the squint-eyed waiter came panting along Greek Street on his second lap.

'I hope he doesn't think it's the finishing tape,' said Detective Inspector Wills, climbing out of the police car that had brought him all of two hundred yards from the lesbian club he had been investigating. 'You seem to have got here double sharp, James, or was you just passing?'

'Heard something was going on while we were down at the Blue Note,' said James carefully. Alex offered silent thanks that he had not dropped him in it.

'Oh, yes, who from?' asked the detective guilelessly. Behind him, a more junior-looking plain-clothes man took out a notebook. Oh, fook. They weren't going to get one past this crafty bugger.

'Someone who'd just come into the club,' volunteered Barry Chilton rashly. Trying to be helpful, he was, but the silly sod was only digging them further in.

'Name?'

'I don't know his name. Never seen him before.'

'But it's a members-only club, Barry. Was he on his own? Did he sign the book?'

'I couldn't say.'

'Well, it's easy enough to find out.' Detective Inspector Wills nodded an instruction to his junior, who made a note. 'The Blue Note's very fussy about these things, unlike some clubs I could name. So what did he tell you exactly, Barry?'

'Just that there'd been a murder in Hog Court.'

'A murder in Hog Court, eh? Now what can have put that idea into his head, exactly?'

Alex felt himself sweating and hoped it wasn't visible. Barry Chilton tugged at his beard and permitted himself an embarrassed grin. 'Well, hasn't there been?'

'I'm asking the questions for the present, son.' A uniformed sergeant came out from Hog Court, which was now brilliantly lit with arc lamps, and murmured something to the detective inspector, who nodded. Something about the doctor wanting a word. Too late for the blurry doctor, reflected Alex, but he supposed they had to go through the motions.

Detective Inspector Wills turned to James Flood. 'You're still going down to the Waiters Club? Wait for me down there, would you?'

'You'll be making a statement, will you, Benny?'

'No, James, you will.'

The threesome skulked off sheepishly towards Shaftesbury Avenue. Passing a line of parked police cars, Alex spotted old Else sitting in the back seat of one of them, with yet another plain-clothes man who was making notes. More to the point, she spotted him too and, for once recognising him, waved, before resuming what was presumably her statement. All Alex needed.

Gerrard Street, looking like a Chinese film set with its pagoda telephone booths, paper lanterns and shopfronts stuffed with Far Eastern bric-à-brac and restaurant signs making no concessions to English, was new territory to Alex. It was like being in blurry Shanghai, he told himself, although having no conception of what blurry Shanghai might look like. The few men – there were no women, not even hookers – drifting in and out of the narrow doorways of what James told him were gambling clubs were all Chinese.

One of these shabby doorways turned out to be the unmarked entrance to the Waiters Club, and it was here that Alex, hovering while James pressed the entryphone button, had an inspired idea.

'Look, lads, if you don't mind, I think I'm gunner sit this one out. I've supped enough for one day and I reckon it's time I was hitting the road.' The tube must be running again by now, or if it wasn't it soon would be. Go as far north as possible on that Northern line, then start hitching lifts.

'Doing a runner, are we?' said Barry Chilton nastily. He could be a belligerent bugger on the quiet.

'No, why should I, what have I got to run away from?' demanded Alex with fine indignation.

'Detective Inspector Wills,' said James Flood.

Oh, well, worth a try. Alex found himself being escorted – hustled, he could have said – down the standard rickety stairs into the standard rickety basement room, furnished with the standard fire-sale cheap Formica-covered tables and wobbly cane chairs. There was a bamboo bar, obviously bought from some failed establishment similar to the one they were in, dispensing cans of beer, dishes of China tea and soft drinks. At the far end of the room a bunch of Chinese kitchen staff, still in their uniform of blue cotton chequered trousers and soiled white bibs, were playing some kind of Oriental dominoes. Three or four Italian waiters, slouched at separate tables, shouted to one another in rough dialects across the smoke-wreathed room. A couple of taxi drivers drank mugs of coffee over early editions of the tabloids. Christ, was it tomorrow already?

James had got the beers in. 'Sorry, Alex,' he said firmly. 'But before Barry and I get dragged any further into this, you're going to have to come clean to Benny Wills.'

'Come clean about what?' demanded Alex, aggrieved. 'I haven't spoken a word to the bugger. It was you two doing all the talking. Why,' aggressively, to Barry Chilton, 'did you have to tell him that someone came in and said there'd been a murder in Hog Court?'

'Because they did,' pointed out Barry Chilton. 'It was yow, kid.'

Well, if he wanted to put it like that. Nonetheless: 'So why did you both take it into your heads to cover up for me? I didn't ask you to.'

'You didn't ask us not to,' said James Flood. 'You're in Soho, Alex. Nobody ever gives anything away about anybody, firm principle. It's like being in Wormwood Scrubs. Grasses unwelcome. Why do you think it's so difficult to do my job on this beat?'

It seemed to Alex that James enjoyed saying 'on this beat'. Touch of the Humphrey Bogarts.

'Yow can't say you haven't got a story today, anyway,' said Barry.

'True, and I've got to write the swine and make it good,' said the Soho correspondent of the *Examiner*. 'So talk among yourselves for half an hour, will you?'

'Bit late to get it in the *Examiner* this morning, isn't it, Jas?' asked Alex, anxious to be friendly. 'So what's the hurry?'

'Who said anything about the *Examiner*? This is going to the *Evening Standard*, first edition.'

Alex whistled. 'Christ on crutches, she'll have your balls for breakfast!'

'How d'you spell transvestite?' asked James Flood, formerly of the *Examiner*, smugly.

'Cross-dresser,' said Barry Chilton.

While the two supernumaries to the reporter's work exchanged aimless chitchat, Alex allowed his mind to drift back to the cock-up they had made between them of the interview with Detective Inspector Wills, and from that to the subject of the interview herself. Himself, he should say. Poor cow. Or poor sod as it would translate a few hours hence, when London read James's story. Alex had the greatest difficulty in thinking of Christine as a man – which, he told himself, was how Christine would have wanted it.

Who would have wanted, wished, needed to murder her, and in such a vicious way? There was that little runt he'd seen scuttering out of Hog Court, but he hadn't looked as if he had anything to do with Christine's crowd. Christine's crowd, though – what was that? Lotter cross-dressers like herself, few gays, maybe some young guy wet behind the ears who'd taken a shine to her, like Alex himself. Could be wunner them *crimes passionel* you used to read about. Or it could be that she'd been up to a bit of cock-teasing and it'd got out of hand. How would Alex know? It was as much not his world as it wasn't that little bloke's. None of it was his world. He wanted to go home. He hoped the police weren't about to give him a hard time, for after all he'd done nothing, only left old Else to carry whatever can there was to be carried.

These ruminations were brought to a halt by the abrupt cessation of the Chinese domino game. 'It's all gone quiet over there,' murmured James, looking up from his notes. No one had come down yet – it must have been instinct. Then Alex noticed the barman adjusting an overhead angled mirror that clearly gave him a view of the stairs and landing. He would have given the Chinese gamblers the nod. As betting counters were scooped into pockets, Detective Inspector Wills and the other plain-clothes man who had been making notes earlier slowly came down the stairs, taking them one at a time as they solicitously helped old Else to descend. Oh, fook. Alex was in for it now.

'So which one of them was it, Else?' asked Detective

Inspector Wills as he and his sidekick took the adjoining table.

Else, remaining standing, peered myopically at the three and then pointed a grimy finger at Alex. 'This young gentleman here. I'm very sorry, young man, but you shouldn't have run away like that, it was very naughty of you. Now if you'll all excuse me, I really must go and have a widdle.'

'Now then, James,' said Detective Inspector Wills heavily, lighting a cigarette. 'I'm going to allow you to bribe Sergeant Bone and I with a cold Tiger beer apiece, then we'll get down to the nitty-gritty.'

Oh, shite. So this was it, then. What was the offence? Withholding vital evidence or what?

He would soon know. The beers arrived. The detective inspector raised a can to his lips. 'Cheers. Now I could have the three of you nailed to the cross, you realise that, don't you? Wasting police time. Making false statements.' He glared at Barry. 'And in your case, Barry Chilton, trying to fuck up my case – a very serious charge indeed.' In a vicious mockery of the poet's Birmingham accent, he mimicked: '"Ow, sumone cyme into the Blue Nowt and said there'd been a murder, but Oi down't know who it was." I could have had four men tied up all night on that wild-goose chase, do you know that?'

'Sorry, Benny,' mumbled Barry.

'So what the fuck were you playing at?'

'He was shielding me,' Alex thought he'd better say.

'Shielding you from what, son?'

'Well, he knew I wanted to get back up to Leeds today, so he was trying to keep me out of it.'

'The nearest you're going to get to Leeds today, my young friend, is Vine Street police station. Now this

162

Christopher or Christine Yardley, as we'll go on calling her. How well did you know her?'

'I didn't know her at all.' Well, it was true. Just because he'd bought her a drink, it didn't mean to say he knew her.

'Never seen her before?'

'No, never,' said Alex recklessly. He saw James Flood frown, and remembered how he must have seen him rushing after Christine from the pub in the belief it was Selby.

'So you didn't see her in any of these pubs and clubs you've been gallivanting around all night?'

'Not that I can remember.' And oh, shite, this Detective Sergeant Bone was writing it all down.

'Oh, you'd remember all right. Everyone remembered our Christine. Now what about old Else? How well do you know her?'

'I don't know her either. I've only been here a day, remember.'

'But she seems to know you.'

'We exchanged a few words at a book-launch do, that's all.'

Detective Inspector Wills nodded to Detective Sergeant Bone, who withdrew from the voluminous valise he had lugged down the stairs – what was that, then, the famous murder bag you read about? – a copy of *The Light and the Shade: The Chiaroscuro Life of Augustus John*. Oh, shite upon shite.

'This was found near the body. Else says she put it down on the ground while she had a pee. She also says you bought it for her. Is that true?'

'I did buy it for her as it happens, yes.' His good deed. Would it earn him Brownie points?

Would it bollox. 'Twenty-nine pounds ninety-five pee, call it thirty quid. Do you make a habit of giving thirty-quid books to women you don't know?'

'No, I suppose I just took a shine to her.'

'You took a shine to her. That incontinent old bag has got to be a hundred and ten years old, son. Have you taken a shine to many women since you got down here, Alex?'

'Not really, no.'

'And you find it easy to spare a sum like thirty pounds, do you? Did you pay in cash or credit card?'

'Cash. I don't have any credit cards, I'm a student.'

'A student who gives away thirty-pound books. Are you sure you didn't nick it?'

'No, course I didn't nick it, Else must have the receipt.'

'So how much cash did you bring down with you from Leeds, Alex?'

'Fifty pounds, why?' Oh, Christ, trap.

'And how much have you got left? Let's have a look in your pockets.'

Alex fished in his pockets with no idea, by this time, what he'd find there. A crumpled twenty-pound note, a ten, a five, and some loose silver.

'So after a day and a night on the piss in Soho, and buying a complete stranger a thirty-quid book, you finish up with nearly as much money as you set off with. How does that come about, then, apart from ducking your round?'

'I don't know.'

'Have a guess.'

'Somebody gave me some dosh.'

'Who?'

'Brendan Barton,' said Alex, scarlet-faced. He felt,

rather than saw, for his eyes were upon the floor, James Flood and Barry Chilton giving him what were called in his part of the world long looks.

'You seem to have met some highly interesting people today, Alex. You should have quite a Christmas-card list this year.'

Mercifully the interrogation was interrupted by the emergence of Else from the ladies', shrilly haranguing the barman: 'Do you know there's no toilet paper in that loo? What a disgrace! I've had to dab myself with some private correspondence.'

Detective Inspector Wills got to his feet. 'Come along, Else, we'll give you a ride home, we don't want you wandering the streets when there's a murderer about. But I don't want you wetting your knickers in the back seat.'

'Oh dear, I'm afraid it's too late for that, Inspector,' said Else coyly, lowering her eyes.

The detective inspector instructed Detective Sergeant Bone: 'Ask the barman for the lend of a tea-towel. And tell him if he doesn't boil it when he gets it back, I'll have the environmental health officer down here.'

So was that it, then? No, was it heckers like. Detective Inspector Wills turned back to Alex.

'I've a lot more questions to ask about how you slot into this business, Alex, but I've got other fish to fry just now. Where are you going to be kipping down?'

'I don't know, I haven't made any arrangements.'

'Not sleeping rough, are we?'

Why, was that an offence? Alex could see himself in a police cell if he didn't play his cards right.

'He can stop with me if he likes,' said Barry Chilton helpfully. Kind of him, but what did he want?

'Where's that, Barry, the Ritz? No, I don't even want

to know where you're staying. Just have him on parade after breakfast, fail not. If he does a runner, I shall be making a very keen inspection of the ashtray arrangements at the Blue Note tonight, got that?'

'So what time do you want to see me?' asked Alex.

'I don't know, son, I haven't got my appointments diary about my person. We'll send for you.'

'How will you know where to find me?'

'Oh, we'll find you all right. You're in Soho.'

Alex did wish people would stop telling him that. Where did they think he supposed himself to be? Fookin Buenos Aires?

'This is an island you're on, son. Oxford Street up there, Charing Cross Road down there, Regent Street that way, Coventry Street that way, there's no way off it without I know about it. Soho Island.'

'Just like Alcatraz,' said James Flood sycophantically.

'Yes, with the great difference that on Alcatraz the sharks are all offshore. Come on, Else – now are you sure you don't want another wee-wee before we go?'

'I'll just see,' said Else, toddling off towards the ladies'. 'Better safe than sorry.'

Alex had never had breakfast out in his life. If you were at home, your mother made it. If you were in a bed-sit, you made it yourself, or the girl-friend did. If you were on holiday, it was the all-in buffet, wasn't it? Failing that, you ate a doughnut on the hoof.

What you didn't do was to go to a caffy. Complete waster money. Yet here he was in the Patisserie Valerie on Old Compton Street, wolfing down a croissant and slurping cappuccino. Very Parisian, not that he had ever set foot in Paris, but he imagined it must be much like this at breakfast time, though more out of doors. The room was buzzing. Shared tables, people passing little jam-pots backwards and forwards, bit like a student refectory really. A student lot in fact they seemed to be mainly: James had told him there was an art school nearby. Foreigners mostly, some fanciable chicks, could be a good pick-up joint. He wished Selby were here.

Apart from that, and apart from the threatened cloud of Detective Inspector Wills's resumed interrogation hanging over him, Alex was feeling ridiculously euphoric. He imagined that under it he must be well shagged out, considering that he'd had no sleep whatever after what Barry Chilton had told him about where they'd put their heads down for a couple of hours upon leaving the Waiters Club.

Parting company with James Flood who had to finish

his story on the Hog Court murder and phone it through to the *Evening Standard*, Barry Chilton had led Alex back along Old Compton Street to Compton's Yard, where they found themselves outside the derelict building next to Stephan Dance's porn shop. It had begun to rain again.

'As Benny Wills would put it, it's not exactly the Ritz,' explained Barry unnecessarily as they skirted the ruin. 'But it's cheaper, although you'll find there's no room service.'

They rounded the building to a narrow alleyway backing on to, although Alex did not know one street from another, Romilly Street. The windows had been bricked up with breeze-blocks, and where the back door had been was sealed off with a stout arrangement of what looked like railway sleepers, as impregnable, it would seem, as any castle keep.

'Now what?' asked Alex, turning up his collar. It was raining seriously now, in fact it was blurry pissing it down.

With a wink, Barry Chilton rubbed the tips of his fingers together in the manner of a safe-breaker. He then quite gently pushed at the middle of the five upright sleepers protecting the doorway. The sleeper edged ajar. A shove of the shoulder and it swung open like a secret panel, which effectively was what it was.

'It's a good job yow's as skinny as a slice of Melba toast,' said Barry, for the gap he had created was no more than seven or eight inches across. 'Let me gow first, then yow can give me a shove in case I get stuck. And watch where you put your feet when you follow me.'

'Why, is it fuller dog-shit?'

No, a better reason than that: there were no floorboards. And a ten-foot drop to the rubble-filled basement. Alex wondered how Barry got on when he arrived home pissed in the dark.

But there was a staircase, much of it intact. The pair

picked their way across the skeleton of joists where the floor had been and, with no banister rail to hang on to, gingerly made it to the upper storey.

This had a floor, but what it lacked was a ceiling. The rain was now bucketing down. Alex flattened himself against the wall, shivering, but there was no shelter. Like the floor downstairs, what was left of the roof consisted only of beams or joists.

'Well, this isn't going to be a barrel of laughs, Barry,' he felt bound to say.

'No probs, kid,' responded Barry cheerfully. 'Just so long as yow down't mind roughing it.'

Alex now saw that there was what had been an iron fire-exit door leading to whatever was on the other side of it. The past tense was appropriate, for it was now padlocked. Christ – that must be directly above Stephan Dance's porn emporium next door. What a place to choose for a pad. Still, with an address like that there should be little fear of burglars.

The padlock snapped open easily, without the aid of a key or even a bent hairpin. 'Rust,' explained Barry. 'Anyway, who's gowing to risk his neck coming up to this dump?'

He swung the door open and in the chilly light of post-dawn Alex saw not the simple bed-sitter he had been expecting but what was evidently a storeroom or stock-room, lined with rough wooden shelves on which were stacked cardboard boxes and brown paper parcels. Peering into a box at random Alex saw that it was filled with grotesque black dildoes. The next one with vibrators. The next with novelty rhubarb-flavoured ribbed condoms. He wondered if Dave's boss back in South Higginshaw was on to this market. The next with X-rated video cassettes: *Millie and Tillie Learn the Hard Way; Nymphette Nuns;*

Wet Nurses. Yeh yeh yeh yeh, you could get all this in Leeds if you had more money than sense.

Considering the prices this stuff fetched, he wondered that Stephan Dance bothered to sub-let his top room. Still, they were miserly buggers, these porn kings. Noted for it.

'So where do you kip down?' he asked, looking round in expectation of at least a sleeping-bag, which he trusted Barry would not be expecting him to share.

'On the floor,' said Barry. 'I used to get my head down on that bottom shelf there, but he's just filled it up with a new consignment of porn mags. Useful if yow want to wank yourself to sleep.'

'And what does he charge you for using this place? As you rightly say, the Ritz it ain't.'

Barry Chilton guffawed. 'Charge me? Charge me? Yow down't think he knows I come up here, dow yow? Be your age, kid.'

Christ on crutches. 'You know what he'll do to you, don't you, Barry, if he catches you up here?'

'I down't like to think about it, it makes my eyes water. But he won't. He hardly ever gets here till after ten and I'm long gone by then.'

'What do you mean by hardly ever?' asked Alex nervously.

'Once in a blue moon he comes in early to cook the books, but touch wood I've always heard the Roller out in the yard and done a quick runner across the wall into Romilly Street. Now yow'd better get some shut-eye, because this could just be one of those mornings,' added Barry mischievously. 'G'night, kid.'

Alex did not sleep at all, or even try to. By eight thirty he was off the premises, leaving Barry Chilton dozing fitfully, his head on a parcel of porn. Barry had told him that he could get a shit-shave-and-shower in the Piccadilly Circus tube-station gents', so that was where he headed first, on the assumption that Piccadilly Circus was not off limits so far as Detective Inspector Wills was concerned.

The streets were already busy, the shops opening, shutters coming down, the cafés filling up. You couldn't even get a cupper tea in Leeds at this timer day. Punctuating the comings and goings, there seemed to be casually dressed men loitering on every corner. They couldn't all be plain-clothes officers, for Chrissake. Was he being followed? A CCTV camera mounted over a sandwich shop swivelled as he ambled along Old Compton Street. Was Detective Inspector Wills, or one of his minions, tracking him?

This was getting ridiculous. He had a good mind to jump on a bus and just bugger off out of it, call Wills's bluff. Trouble was, there seemed to be no bus service in So-oh, and he was buggered if he was going to take a taxi, even if he knew where he wanted to go.

He wandered on, turning up Wardour Street and then into Berwick Street. In Walkers Court a couple of shysters were already setting up an orange box for a Find the Lady game. Nah nah nah, been there, done that, you didn't catch Alex out again with that one, and anyway they were probably plain-clothes men.

The rain clouds had cleared away leaving the streets bright and fresh-smelling in the early sunlight. The fresh smell, it proved, was a medley of ground coffee, newly baked bread, and the fruit and veg on the Berwick Street market stalls. The pungent odours gave the morning air a whiff of anticipation, but Alex couldn't say he went a bundle on Berwick Street Market, it wasn't a patch on the great glass-covered market up in Leeds. Seemed to him they didn't know what a blurry market was down here, although he could have done with wunner them thick bacon sarnies that so many of the stallholders were getting their teeth into.

Hunger drove Alex op. Dodging the electric dustcart methodically mopping up the cabbage leaves, he meandered on until the cries of the market traders were distant sounds eventually drowned by traffic. Now he was in Broadwick Street, Lexington Street, Brewer Street with its vintage magazine store – big plastic statuette of Ringo he would've bought for Selby if he had any money and knew where she was – and thus, having come full circle without realising it, back to Old Compton Street. Seemed to be the centre of the blurry world round these parts, Old Compton Street did.

The aroma of Jamaican Blue Mountain wafting out of the Algerian Coffee Stores reminded him of the need for breakfast, so presently he established himself in Patisserie Valerie. This was the life, eh? He could really take to this caffy lark. They could do with wunner these places in Leeds – all they had was blurry Starbucks.

Finishing his croissant and mopping up the crumble of buttery flakes, he reached for the freebie newspaper that was lying across the table. *Metro* – yeh yeh yeh, they had something of the sort in Leeds. SOHO MURDER. MAN DRESSED AS WOMAN SLASHED IN ALLEY. By James Flood.

Jesus. That editress of his on the *Examiner* would have his guts for garters. Alex could almost smell the stench of fat sizzling in the fire.

He was wondering whether the dwindling budget would run to another cappuccino – pleasant though the prospect was, you practically had to take out a mortgage to get a cupper coffee down here – when into the café walked Ellis Hugo Bell of Bell Famous Productions. He was wearing

172

dark glasses: nothing unusual about that, but normally he sported them on the top of his head while today he had them clamped firmly over his eyes. As he came nearer Alex saw why: he was trying to disguise a swollen, purple eye that looked as if he had done twelve rounds at the old Great Windmill Street gymnasium. The split lip and the grazed cheekbone he could unfortunately do nothing about.

Alex grinned. With what he imagined to be the Soho insider's crafty knowingness he said: 'Your mate Kim Grizzard finally catch up with you, did he?'

'Wait till I catch up with *him*!' snarled Bell. 'Where's Simon, I mean James Flood? Have I got a story for him!'

'He's already got a story. I expect he's with that Detective Inspector Wills.'

'Yeah, well, this is a better one.'

Despite having been duffed up, it was plain that Bell had something to be pleased with himself about. His hand hovered over his inside pocket until, with simulated reluctance, he withdrew a bulky and official-looking letter on several typed pages of classy-looking A4.

'If you do see Simon, James rather, tell him about this and say he'll find me in the French, getting well trolleyed.'

Arts Council of England. In further response to your application of blah blah blah, the Arts Council has now had the opportunity to consider in depth your proposal for blah blah blah. Alex didn't have to read it all, couldn't in fact, for it was more soporific than any exam dissertation he'd ever flammed together. Luckily Bell had marked two passages in yellow highlight. The first said that the project as described in Appendix I would qualify for a National Lottery grant of £12,500 (twelve thousand five hundred pounds only) provided always that he could match said sum by such and such a date. The second said that the grant was also conditional upon whatever doorway in which he mounted his rostrum camera possessing or being provided with approved wheelchair access.

'How do you raise the other half, then?' asked Alex, playing the canny Yorkshireman.

'Easy-peasy. This letter is bankable.'

'So you're in business?'

'Of course I'm in business. I always was in business. Never a shadow of doubt about it. Don't you wish now you'd bought one of those hundred-pound seed-money units, because as of today the price is two-fifty?'

'I thought that was for the other thing – what was it called again?'

'*Kill Me Nicely*, working title. First draft script by Kim Grizzard, after some discussion. The poor bastard couldn't write fuck in the dust on a Venetian blind but at least he'll give me something to work on. No, I shall do them as a twin project. No reason to bother the Lottery Fund with the small print. *Walk On By* will seed-capitalise *Kill Me*. *Kill Me* will capitalise *Walk On By*. With this letter,' crowed Bell, brandishing it before stuffing it back in his pocket, 'I'm laughing and giggling.'

It all sounded a bit dodgy to Alex but what did he know? He was trying to think of a way of sliding that question of seed-money units back into the conversation – well, his grandma had after all left him five hundred in Premium Bonds and they had earned him sod-all so far – when both he and Bell became aware of something of a commotion outside.

Numbers of people were hurrying purposefully along Old Compton Street, as if late for an appointment. Alex knew a good sprinkling of them, if only by sight. There went Brendan Barton waddling by, huffing and puffing from the exertion of a departure from his usual leisurely gait. There were the two flymen. There was Jenny Wise, minus the soap opera star who was clearly by now yesterday's man. There was the shit-hot jazz piano player from Gerry's Club in the spade hat. And who was that, scurrying past? Her with the bum? No, it wasn't Selby, do leave it out, Ali. Fifth time he'd spotted her this morning.

But there, unaccompanied for once by his claque of Japanese or American tourists, went Len Gates. Barry Chilton, running a battery razor over his chin as he hurried along. Half the riff-raff and flotsam and jetsam of the pubs and clubs of Soho Alex had half noticed on last night's crawl. Old Else, helped along by James Flood, who as he glanced into the gateau-laden windows of Patisserie Valerie saw Alex and Bell and peeled off to enter the café, leaving Else to hobble along unaided in the rear of the great Old Compton Street exodus. Alex was reminded of some late-night old movie with the townsfolk marching on the sheriff's office.

'What the hell are you two doing in here swigging coffee?' demanded James, for Bell, in his munificence, had ordered two small espressos.

'I want you!' exclaimed Bell. 'Got a story for you.'

'Bollox – you're taking part in a story. Free drinks over at Mabel's. Official.'

'What's that?' asked Alex sharply. Free drinks over at Mabel's, on whatever pretext, were just what he needed. While awaiting Detective Inspector Wills's summons, he could spend the morning joining Ellis Hugo Bell in getting quietly trolleyed.

'The New Kismet,' expanded James. 'Mabel's cracked up at last. Drinks on the house.'

175

'But why?' Bell was genuinely bewildered at the concept of something for nothing.

'Seems she's suddenly decided to give Soho the elbow. Taking herself off to Brighton. Soho by the Sea. Good tale for the *Standard*. Come on, before those bastards drink the place dry.'

They had difficulty getting into the New Kismet Club, by reason of the hordes trying to shove their way down the stairs. 'If the fire inspector sees this little lot, she'll lose her licence for sure,' said a concerned James Flood as they edged and squeezed their way through the throng.

'No probs,' said one of the two flymen, just ahead of them. 'He's down there already, on double rums.'

The New Kismet, when they had fought their way into it, was a heaving mass of Soho humanity or in some cases sub-humanity. Jenny Wise had positioned herself behind the bar where she was dispensing trebles with both hands, passing whisky bottles to such as preferred them. Mabel herself, wearing a smart outdoor coat, had clambered up on to a rocky bar stool, from which perilous position she was separating sheep from goats.

'All right, a good half of you can piss off this minute. It's members only, members only, get back to the Coach and Horses where you belong. Don't serve that little toerag, Jen, he's no more a member than I'm Joan of fucking Arc. Are you a member, sir? Go on, then, fuck off, sling your hook.' She glared down at Alex as he struggled to the bar with James Flood. 'You're not a member for a kick-off, sir. Go on, fuck off.'

'I joined yesterday, Mabel,' lied Alex, regarding himself by now as well versed in Soho drinking club ways. 'Don't you remember?'

'Oh, yes,' riposted Mabel. 'And don't you remember me barring you for life? Off you go – fuck off.'

'He's with me, Mabel,' put in James Flood diplomatically.

'Is he? In that case he's double barred. No, hang about – it's Jamesy, isn't it? In that case you're both life members. I've got a good column for you, Jamesy. End of an era. Queen of the drinking clubs says fuck Soho. I'm selling up, fucking off to Brighton. Soho by the Sea.'

'So I'm told, Mabel. Do you want to do an interview?'

'Make it up, darling, I've got a train to catch. Now be sure to lock up, Jen, when they've drunk the place dry. Drinks on the house, everybody, members only. All the rest of you can fuck off.'

'I wish you'd get down off that bar-stool, Mabel, you're going to break your neck before you've finished,' urged Jenny Wise.

'It's my neck to break, now pass me up another gin and I'll be on my merry way. You, sir – you're not a member, not even of the human fucking race. Go on, off you fuck!'

'Now before you go, Mabel, are you quite sure I can't make you an appointment with someone else?' asked Jenny, sounding concerned.

'What – second opinion style of thing? I've had a second and a third and a fourth opinion. I've had more opinions than the fucking *Brains Trust*, my darling, and they all say the same thing. It's the tests, see, Jen. What can't speak can't lie.'

'All I can say, Mabel, is one time I thought I had all the symptoms, but at the death it turned out to be a dose.'

'In your place, Jen, that would have been the first thing I thought of.'

As the two women, Mabel still perched up on her swaying bar stool like a squawking parrot on top of its cage, continued to exchange these intimacies as uninhibitedly as if they were talking privately over a cup of tea, Alex began to feel acutely embarrassed. He had only the sketchiest idea what they were rabbiting on about but it seemed to him that it was nonner his business. He shoved his way along the bar to where Ellis Hugo Bell was flourishing his Arts Council letter at Brendan Barton. In passing he brushed against Len Gates who, clutching an unaccustomed large Scotch, was holding forth to the two flymen on the history of Soho's contribution to the West End theatre, in the mistaken belief that they would be remotely interested.

'Now with the demolition of the slums in the late 1880s to create Shaftesbury Avenue, no fewer than five new theatres were to be built between Great Windmill Street and Cambridge Circus. The first of these was the Lyric, constructed in 1888 . . .'

'Wossat pub backer the Lyric?' the first flyman asked the second flyman. 'Stage doorkeeper goes in there.'

'Dunno, mate, never use it. Lyric Tavern would it be?'

'Nah, that's in Great Windmill Street. Lyric Tavern you're thinking of, we shudder taken Old Jakie in there, he sometimes went in the Lyric Tavern.'

'Now the Lyric Tavern,' said Len Gates, effortlessly resuming control of the reins, 'retains its very fine original Victorian tiling . . .'

Alex found Ellis Hugo Bell of Bell Famous Productions still crowing to a sceptical Brendan Barton. He had taken a gamble on Brendan Barton having forgotten the little matter of the fifty pounds he owed him. So it proved. There was no signal, indeed, that Brendan had any idea who he was. Soho's collective amnesia had a lot to be said for it.

'If the idea was such a bummer,' Bell was bragging, 'would the Arts Council cough up twelve and a half grand?'

'Of course they would. The Arts Council would cough up twelve and a half grand for a barrowload of horse manure. Indeed, I believe they've been known to do so.'

'You'll see,' said Bell complacently. 'Once *Walk On By* gets its own website it'll become a cult thing.'

'Yes, well, don't be a cult all your life,' quipped Brendan.

A stranger to Alex, a civilian as James Flood would have described him, that is, not one of the Soho faction, had been listening inquisitively to these exchanges. Guzzling whisky, he was already, so Alex judged, three parts cut.

'Excuse me, but I couldn't help overhearing your conversation,' he began.

'Yes you could,' returned Brendan Barton. 'You could have positioned yourself five feet away. Or for preference, in the next parish.'

The stranger smiled weakly, uncertain whether to take offence or not. He ploughed on: 'Only I recognise your voice. You're him, aren't you? That Brendan Barton?'

'Not necessarily,' said Brendan warily.

'Do you mind if I ask you a question, Brendan?' said the intruder with offensive familiarity. 'Where did it all go wrong?'

Brendan shook his head regretfully. 'You're in the wrong joke, sir. That story goes better with George Best in it.'

The stranger turned to Alex and Bell and jerked his head towards Brendan Barton. 'To say he's a has-been, he's a cocky bugger, your mate, isn't he?'

Both Alex and Bell wisely elected to ignore the question, but Brendan said evenly: 'Better a cocky bugger than a cunt.'

The stranger scowled, then knocked back his drink in

an aggressively determined manner. 'What was that you just called me?'

'Hearing bad too, is it? You are mortally afflicted.'

'Do you want to come outside and repeat it?'

'Why – are the acoustics better out there?'

Pleased with his rejoinder, Brendan Barton raised his glass high, signalling to Jenny behind the bar the need for a refill. His day was shaping up nicely. But then, reflected Alex enviously, every day must be an adventure for this bugger.

While the civilian, as Alex now thought of him, struggled for something cutting to say, Mabel had been helped down from her bar stool by James Flood. Taking possession of her commodious handbag, she now reached out and removed the stranger's empty glass from his grasp.

'You're barred. You're so fucking barred you must've been born fucking barred. Go on. Out.'

'That wouldn't be a subtle hint, would it, Mabel?' blustered the civilian. 'I'll just have the one and then I'll be on my merry way.'

'You've already had the one, and that was one too many. And don't be so fucking familiar. Piss off out of it, I shan't tell you again.'

'Curiously enough, Mabel,' said Brendan, 'this gentleman was only just now inviting me to join him outside for a little alfresco tête-à-tête. I should be only too happy to oblige, if that would help.'

'You stay where you are, Brendan, I'll see the toerag off myself. Take care, one and all, and don't set the fucking place on fire.'

Shepherding the civilian ahead of her, evidently prepared to frogmarch him out if necessary, Mabel made for the stairs to a chorus, instigated by Brendan Barton, of 'For She's A Jolly Good Fellow'.

As the singing died raggedly away, Mabel's strident voice could be heard from the doorway above: 'Yes, madam, what can I do you for?'

'Would you move out of my way, please?'

'No, I fucking will not. This is a private club, members only.'

'Yes, I know it's a private club, and I've got enough on you to have it closed down tomorrow. Don't you know who I am?'

Oh, fook. Her. Alex knew that voice, and more particularly so did James. He had gone white.

'If I were you, mate, I'd duck into the bog and stay there,' advised Alex.

'Can't. Else is in there.'

In any case, it was too late. Jane Rich, the editor of the *Examiner*, was fast gaining ground.

'I have to speak urgently to James Flood of the *Examiner*. I'm his editor.'

'He's not here.'

'I happen to know he is, and there must be about seventy witnesses to the fact down there. Since you're only supposed to accommodate a maximum of forty, I suggest you stop fucking me about and let me pass.'

It was, Alex judged, Jane's command of four-letter words that won the day for her. At any rate, she was soon bounding down the stairs, brandishing a copy of the *Evening Standard* first edition.

CROSS-DRESS KILLING IN SOHO. By James Flood. This was it, then. Alex Singer was very glad he was not James Flood.

Yet despite some trembling and nervous swallowing,

James seemed comparatively unfazed as Jane Rich, cutting a swathe through the crowded room, bore down on him.

'I am going to sue you for breach of contract and the *Evening Standard* for breach of copyright,' she announced at the top of her voice. 'The same goes for *Metro*. Also I hope you have some other string to your bow, James Flood, because I shall see to it personally that you never work in Fleet Street again. Now just what the fuck do you think you're playing at?'

'Bit late for all that, Jane,' said James with controlled smugness. 'I've joined the *Evening Standard*.'

'You're in no position to join the *Evening Standard*. You haven't worked out your notice.'

'I don't have to give notice, Jane. I was on three months' trial, remember?'

'You're still on three months' trial. And when it's up, you're fired.'

'I don't think so, Jane, I looked up my letter of appointment. The three months expired,' said James with great satisfaction, 'at midnight last night.'

It was a line he had obviously been rehearsing and rerehearsing in his head, and he delivered it perfectly. Jane Rich gaped, opened and closed her mouth several times, goldfish fashion, and then turned on her heel.

As she clattered up the stairs, Detective Sergeant Bone made his way down them. He did not bother to push his way into the room. With jabbing motions he indicated Alex, James Flood and Barry Chilton. The jerk of his head said: 'The guvnor wants all three of you. Now.'

11

Those with nothing better to do with their time – perhaps the majority of Soho dwellers on this bright morning – were beginning to line the streets in readiness for the annual Waiters' Race. Detective Inspector Wills should have been standing by as one of the judges, but had had to cry off due to other duties.

Murder, explained Detective Sergeant Bone as his little party picked their way along Gerrard Street, now as thronged as any Hong Kong bazaar, was not usually on the guvnor's beat. But the Division had two men off with stress and another suspended while awaiting the outcome of an inquiry into allegations of causing a trauma to a suspect under questioning, and so there was an under-manning problem. Besides, no one knew the area better than Detective Inspector Wills, so that was that. He had set up his Incident Room in the Waiters Club in Gerrard Street, which was unoccupied during the daytime.

Alex was apprehensive, James quite chirpy, as befitted a reporter who had got two scoops in two papers before noon, and landed himself a good job into the bargain. Barry Chilton's only anxiety was that he had a gig in Swindon that night and wanted to get off.

'Is this going to take long, kid?' he asked Detective Sergeant Bone. 'Only I mean tough luck and all that, but I hardly knew Christine.'

'Shouldn't take more than a few minutes, unless you've

been where you didn't ought to have been,' said Detective Sergeant Bone genially. 'Look on it as a three-man identity parade.'

Which was exactly what it was. For as Alex, James and Barry descended into the Waiters Club, where Detective Inspector Wills sat in the middle of the room poring over a stack of printouts spilling from a computer he had got set up down there, and a uniformed woman constable ploddingly manned a constantly ringing telephone – 'Incident room. No, he's tied up at present, I'm going to have to put you on hold' – the squint-eyed waiter, looking at his watch, or rather looking at a space in the air a foot away from his wrist, awaited their presence. He was wearing a snowy floor-length apron and carrying a tin tray, the badges of the Soho Waiters' Race.

'Good of you to come down, chaps,' said Detective Inspector Wills, as if they had done so voluntarily. Alex supposed that technically they had, but there was no disguising the menace behind Detective Sergeant Bone's affability: he would have the three of them in handcuffs as soon as look at them. 'It's just a question of establishing which of you our friend here saw in the Transylvania Club last night, seeing as how he was signed in under a false name. Whoever it was, was seen later in Hog Court. He knows it was one of you but he couldn't be sure which one of you it was. Never mind, we'll get it sorted out soon enough.'

Shite.

'Now, Piedro, can you positively identify the man who came into the Transylvania with Christine last night?'

'Yes, sair, Meester Inspector Wills, sair.'

'Point him out.'

Unerringly, the squint-eyed waiter jabbed a lungeing index finger towards James Flood.

'Are you sure it was him, Piedro?'

'No, sair, Meester Inspector Wills, sair, not heem. Heem!' The squint-eyed waiter pointed again, this time at Barry Chilton.

'Bollox. I've never set foot in the Transylvania in my life,' protested Barry.

'Quiet! Piedro. Would you go over and touch the shoulder of the man you say you saw in the Transylvania?'

The squint-eyed waiter walked crabwise forward and grabbed the arm of Detective Sergeant Bone.

'You're getting warmer, lad,' said Detective Inspector Wills encouragingly. 'One more try.' Another lunge, and Alex was finally identified.

'Just a last question, Piedro, then you can get off to your Waiters' Race. Who was it you saw lurking around Hog Court last night? Was it one of these three?'

'I wasn't lurking, I was waiting,' protested Alex.

'So you admit you were there?'

'You know I was there.'

'I know what old Else has told me, but so far I haven't heard it from you, son. What were you doing in Hog Court at approximately seven minutes to four this morning?'

Oh, so it was getting official, was it? Approximately seven minutes to four. Watch out, Ali.

'You know – the usual reason.' He tried to sound cocky but it came out shifty.

'There's a lot of usual reasons for going into Hog Court at that hour, from my observation, Alex. For a pee. For a quick shag. For a quiet wank. For a flash. To commit a burglary. To mug somebody. To rape somebody. To commit a murder.'

'For a pee,' answered Alex sullenly.

'And did you ever have this pee?'

Come to think of it, no, he never did.

'No, I was sick instead.'

'They're not alternatives, you know,' said Detective Inspector Wills mildly. To the squint-eyed waiter, who was looking agitated and trying to bring his watch within his flawed line of vision: 'All right, Piedro, off you go. Come back after the race and you can sign your statement. Good luck, and don't run into any lamp-posts.' Then to James Flood and Barry Chilton as the squint-eyed waiter zigzagged to the stairs: 'You two can piss off as well.'

'Any news of the murder weapon, Benny?' asked the new *Evening Standard* reporter.

'A Swiss Army knife has been located on a builders' skip in Greek Street,' said the detective inspector woodenly. 'It has yet to be established as the murder weapon.'

Swiss Army knife. Swiss Army knife. Swiss Army knife.

'Can I use that, Benny?'

'You can if you don't claim the murder was done with the gadget that takes stones out of horses' hooves.'

Swiss Army knife. Where had he seen a Swiss Army knife? Trouble was, last night had become a blur. He had been well pissed for one thing, and for another, lack of sleep was now catching up with him. Swiss Army knife. It would come. It had better do.

With James Flood and Barry Chilton dismissed, Alex felt isolated, the more so because without any prompting Detective Inspector Wills, Detective Sergeant Bone and the woman constable, all of them with notebooks at the ready and, Alex noticed out of the corner of his eye, not one but two tape-recorders surreptitiously going, had drawn up chairs and silently arranged themselves into a semi-circle around him.

'This could be as good a time as any to have that pee you never got round to,' said Detective Inspector Wills encouragingly. 'We might be some time.'

He was right. Alex went out and evacuated his bladder, and had done so, or tried to do so in dribbles, another twice before the interview was at long last over.

'Now the first thing is, Alex, you seem to have got yourself signed in at the Transylvania Club as one Mr D. Singleton, and the waiter who's just identified you says you were addressed by the dead person as David. Why would that be, Alex?'

Shite. How did you explain the inexplicable? Well, before I knew Christine was a bloke, I was entertaining hopes of shagging her, so it was just a natural precaution not to give her my real name. Sort of nominal Durex. That do?

'Well?'

'I don't know. It just looked like the kind of place where it would be a good idea to give a false name. After all, that waiter who's just gone out was calling himself Petra, and if it comes to that, Christine's name wasn't really Christine, was it?'

'That's true, but the pair of them were known all over Soho as Petra and Christine. I've not heard anyone addressing you as David. Except, so we're informed, the dead person.'

'Yes, I introduced myself as David.'

'Why should you want to do that?'

So it went on, for what seemed like hours. Some of Detective Inspector Wills's questions were pointless, some seemingly guileless, some obviously intended to catch him out. The inspector, patiently and ploddingly, was taking him round and round in circles; but Alex could not help noticing that each otherwise repetitive circuit yielded some fresh and, for all he knew, possibly incriminating fragment of information. He had begun to feel very tired, exhausted in fact. Perhaps that was the idea.

Eventually, after he had been encouraged to drink a glass of water as if some physical ordeal were ahead of him, he and Detective Inspector Wills between them cobbled together a statement which was typed up by the constable on an old-fashioned manual portable. It was given to Alex to read through, which he did with blurred and gritty eyes.

His name was Alexander Bernard Singer of 14 Quarry Lane, South Higginshaw, West Yorkshire, LS15 2QR. He also rented a bed-sitter at 5B Station Place in central Leeds. He was a student of media studies at Leeds Metropolitan University.

He had a girl-friend, Sheilagh Lyons, known to her friends as Selby, a probationer nurse at Leeds General Infirmary. They were not engaged. Selby was a town in East Yorkshire. He did not know why she had named herself after an obscure town, and had counselled her against it. After a series of minor quarrels, Selby had decided to come down to London to think things out, as she had put it. He had reason to believe she was in Soho. After two weeks, when he had not heard from her and she was refusing to accept calls on her mobile, he had determined to track her down in London and have it out with her. By have it out he meant establish how he stood with her. He had hitched a lift to London, intending to remain only twenty-four hours, since he had university business in Leeds.

Once in Soho, he had made no serious enquiries about the possibility of Selby's whereabouts, as there did not seem to be any point. He knew that a friend of hers would have told her of his movements, and he felt that if she wished to make herself known to him, she would do so.

He had become acquainted with several interesting people during the day, among them Mr James Flood, a newspaper reporter, who had become something of a drinking companion. Whilst in Mr Flood's company he had thought he had spotted Selby leaving a public house and had run after her. The person had resembled her from the rear but proved not to be her. They had a brief conversation.

During the course of the day he had met Ms Jenny Wise, the actress, with whom he had had sex at her invitation, and Mr Brendan Barton, the television personality, who had given him the sum of two hundred pounds for correctional therapy. He had also met a former model known to him only as Else, who had sat for a famous artist whose name he could no longer remember, and whilst at a book-launch party he had found himself at, he had presented said Else with a volume priced at £29.95. He had no motive in making such a gesture.

Much later in the evening he had been sheltering from the rain in the doorway of what proved to be the Transylvania Club. He did not know it was a transvestite club. He had never himself worn women's clothing, nor had any wish to. In the lobby he met the person he had previously mistaken for his friend Selby – a Ms Christine, or as it would turn out, Mr Christopher Yardley, who invited him into the club, where he was signed in under the name of D. Singleton.

He did not know why he had given a false name, except

that he had thought it was the done thing to give false names in Soho drinking clubs. He had never been in Soho before.

He would admit that in an earlier, informal statement he had erroneously told Detective Inspector Wills that until encountering the body in Hog Court he had never set eyes on Christopher, a.k.a. Christine Yardley, in his life before. He had said this because he did not wish to become involved, since he needed to get back to Leeds. He now realised that withholding information in this manner was an offence.

He could not agree that the reason he had given 'Christine' a false name for himself was because he was hoping to have sexual intercourse with 'her', or failing her consent, that he intended to rape her in Hog Court. It was true that he had hoped to have sexual intercourse with 'Christine' but had gone off the idea when 'she' turned out to be a man. He most certainly was not repelled by the discovery, but he had no idea how to go about having sexual congress with a transvestite. In fact given that he found himself in Soho, he wouldn't have minded finding out.

It was true that what with Ms Jenny Wise and Mr Brendan Barton he had had some interesting sexual encounters during the day and had been hoping for another, but he was not a sexual predator. It was just that not having seen Selby for over two weeks he was feeling sexually frustrated. It had to be remembered that he was a normal young man.

He did not speak to anyone else at the Transylvania Club.

After leaving the Transylvania Club he had gone to meet his friend Mr James Flood at Gerry's Club, by arrangement. He had spoken briefly to Ms Jenny Wise but she had more or less snubbed him. With Mr Flood, he had then gone on to the Blue Note Club. He had not attempted to pick anyone up at the Blue Note Club.

Whilst at the Blue Note Club he had begun to feel melancholy and thought he would attempt to make contact with Selby on his mobile. He had gone out into Greek Street for this purpose but was unable to make contact. Whilst in Greek Street he had felt the need to urinate. Not wishing to go back down into the Blue Note until his mood of depression had passed, he crossed the street to Hog Court.

Together with Ms Else, whom he gathered was in Hog Court with the same intention as himself, he had discovered the body of 'Christine' Yardley.

He was sorry to have left it to Else to explain matters to the police. He supposed he had panicked. He could not think what there was to panic about.

He had never been in Hog Court before that moment. Whilst he had been in many places in Soho during the course of the day, and could not remember them all, he would certainly have remembered having been in Hog Court.

He did not know why he would remember having been in Hog Court. He just knew that he had not been there.

He had not gone back into Hog Court looking for a Swiss Army knife. He did not own a Swiss Army knife, never had done.

If Else had thought she had seen him pick up something whilst he was retching, she was mistaken. He had merely been stooping to see if there was tomato in his vomit, as indeed there was, as always, even though he had had nothing with tomato in it. You could call it research, something to tell the lads back in Leeds. By no means was he picking up a—

Swiss Army knife. Fooking Swiss Army knife! He had got it. Bloke in wunner them boozers last night, out on that pub crawl with James. Same little bloke he had seen slinking out of Hog Court while he was waiting for a pee.

'Describe him,' said Detective Inspector Wills.

Alex described him as best he could.

'And you say he was carrying a folded raincoat.'

'Yes.'

'Describe it.'

'I don't know that I could. It was just a raincoat.'

'But you'd recognise it if you saw it again, yes?'

'I should think so, yes.'

'Yet you can't remember which out of all these pubs you were in last night you saw this guy in?'

'It can only be one of forty-eight, guv,' Detective Sergeant Bone pointed out soothingly. 'Unless they were doing the clubs and wine bars as well, in which case we'll be back with you about next Tuesday.'

'You say James Flood of the *Examiner* was with you on this pub crawl?' said Detective Inspector Wills to Alex.

'Of the *Evening Standard*, now,' said Alex, not without vicarious pride.

'Son, I don't care if he's now on the *Exchange and fucking Mart*. Did he see this bloke with the Swiss Army knife?'

'I don't think so. I think he was talking to the pub landlord.'

'Then let's hope for your sake you can find this mysterious figure again,' said Detective Inspector Wills with an ominous smile. 'Off you go, and don't get pissed.'

As Alex and Detective Sergeant Bone made for the stairs, they were swamped by a human tide flowing down – a horde of over-excited, tin-tray-banging waiters, looking in their crisp ankle-length white aprons like extras in a lithograph by Toulouse-Lautrec. Borne shoulder high by his friends was the squint-eyed waiter, beaming at the wall and brandishing his first prize in the Waiters' Race of a jeroboam of Moët et Chandon.

Alex could have done with a dropper that champagne, even though the muck tickled his nose and made his eyes water – it was thirsty work, answering questions and making statements. Still, he supposed he'd be allowed a drink on this reconstructed pub crawl Detective Sergeant Bone was taking him on, hence the inspector's injunction not to get pissed. He wondered if the Clubs and Vice Squad got a booze allowance. Probably did: it was difficult to see how they could carry out their duties without dipping their hands in their pockets. Especially since, as Alex happened to know, the Old Bill weren't allowed to accept free drinks when on duty.

Oh, weren't they? At their first stop, the Coach and Horses, Detective Sergeant Bone firmly ordered a large Scotch, leaving Alex to pay for it, before taking himself off into a corner for a discreet chat with Norman, the guvnor.

At the French House, where Alex expected the detective to reciprocate, he did nothing of the sort. However, the two flymen were at the bar, and Detective Sergeant Bone very kindly allowed them to buy him his next Scotch. Thank Christ for that: at the rate they were going Alex would soon be broke again, and God only knew when he was going to get out of Detective Inspector Wills's clutches and back on his way to Leeds.

If ever. What did making a statement mean? Once you'd signed it, were you free to go? More than likely not, all the things he'd had to confess to. Not that they were crimes exactly, but looking back over that statement, what he'd been made to put into it, he must have come out of it as if he'd been behaving in a definitely dodgy way. In the inspector's shoes, he certainly wouldn't give himself the green light, not just yet. He wondered if he was going to spend the night in a police cell. If it meant he could get some kip, he wouldn't really mind, so long as it didn't get into the *Yorkshire Evening Post*. No, James Flood would keep it out, they were best mates by now. But he was wishing he'd never set eyes on fookin So-oh. As for blurry Selby, he blamed her for this.

'Your guvnor was right about the fine at Marlborough Street,' the first flyman was saying to Detective Sergeant Bone.

'Twenty quid apiece for taking a dead body on the tube,' said the second flyman. 'Diabolical liberty. If it's really an offence by law, you'd think London Transport would have a fixed penalty.'

'He's usually right about these things,' said Detective Sergeant Bone. 'But if you've just had to fork out forty quid between the pair of you, why aren't you down the New Kismet mopping up the free booze? Don't say they've drunk the place dry already?'

'Nah.' The first flyman waxed philosophical. 'We came out. It's a funny thing about booze, mate. If you don't have to pay for it, it never tastes as good as if you do.'

'Now I've never found that,' said Detective Sergeant Bone, knocking back his Scotch. 'No one you recognise here, Alex? Come on, then, you can buy me one in the Sun and Thirteen Cantons.'

Alex was nearly sure, when they reached the Sun and Thirteen Cantons, that it had not been on James Flood's itinerary last night, but Detective Sergeant Bone insisted that it was one of his regular ports of call, so Alex obediently trotted after him. There, they encountered a bad-tempered Kim Grizzard haranguing the barman: 'But are you sure? It's not good enough just to say you don't think so. Go and ask your boss. This is a very valuable manuscript we're talking about.'

'If it narrows down your search,' said Alex helpfully, 'I think you'll find the Sun and Thirteen Cantons isn't on the list James gave you.'

'I wouldn't know, I left the list in a pub.'

'Like the script of your book,' said Detective Sergeant Bone.

'I didn't leave the bloody script behind, this dozy sod did,' said Grizzard, jabbing Alex in the chest. 'And I'll tell you what I'm doing, list or no list. There are forty-one pubs in Soho, so I've been told.'

'Forty-eight,' amended the detective sergeant.

'And on the principle of leaving no stone unturned, I'm going to try every one of them. And then if that book doesn't surface, I'm going to kick the living shit out of this prat here. Have you seen what I did to that devious ratbag Ellis Hugo Bell?' he enquired of Alex with interest.

'Yeh yeh yeh, he's in a bad way.'

'Compared with what's in store for you, friend, he looks unblemished.'

'Threatening words or behaviour, two-thousand-pound fine and six months,' recited Detective Sergeant Bone. 'You'll find us in the Three Greyhounds, and after that the Blue Posts. Drink up, Alex.'

On the way across to the Three Greyhounds Detective Sergeant Bone's mobile trilled. 'Yes, guv? Dunno, I'll ask him. Colour? Make? Size? I'll get back to you.'

Pocketing the cell-phone, Bone, with a sphinx-like expression, made no reference to the conversation until they were in the pub, with Alex getting them in. War of nerves, Alex reckoned. Well, if the detective sergeant wasn't going to tell him, he wasn't going to ask. Sod him.

But at length Detective Sergeant Bone volunteered: 'That was the guvnor.'

'Oh, yes?' stalled Alex.

'As you'll have gathered.'

'Right.'

Tiring of the stonewalling, Detective Sergeant Bone moved on: 'He wants to know if you came down to London wearing a coat.'

'No.'

'You're sure about that?'

'Course I'm sure. I don't even own a raincoat.'

'Who says we're talking about a raincoat?'

Walked into that one, didn't he? He reckoned they played these little games just to keep themselves on their toes. Ward off boredom. Either that, or they watched too much cops and robbers telly.

'Well, I wouldn't be wearing a top coat at this timer year, would I?'

'So you didn't have a raincoat when you got down here?'

'No, I've told you.'

'But it was pissing down cats and dogs last night, Alex. How did you keep dry if you didn't have a raincoat? I mean that suit you're wearing' – fingering a lapel – 'it's not been wet, now has it?'

'It's all in my statement, how many more times? I was

sheltering in the doorway of the Transylvania Club, which is how I came to meet Christine.'

This was how they got you. It was how they wore you down. They nagged away like a dog at a bone until you didn't know what you were saying, or until you'd say anything for the sake of shutting them up. Although he thought he was on to all their tricks by now, Alex was beginning to feel as if he were being taken on a route march along a tightrope.

'What's your blood group, Alex?'

'No idea – why?'

'I think you know why. What can you tell me about a bloodstained raincoat found under a park bench in Soho Square?'

Alex saw a straw to clutch at. 'Neatly folded, was it?'

'Might've been, why?'

'Because he was carrying a neatly folded raincoat when he came out of Hog Court.'

'Well, let's say somebody was carrying a neatly folded raincoat,' said Bone grudgingly. 'What size d'you take, Alex? Medium?'

'No idea – I've told you, I don't own a raincoat.'

As they progressed from pub to pub, Detective Sergeant Bone having greatly extended the rerun of last night's tour with the seeming intention of covering every one of Soho's forty-eight pubs, their path continued to cross and recross that of Kim Grizzard, who was growing ever more agitated, ever more belligerent and ever more drunk.

There had been no sign of anyone resembling the owner of the Swiss Army knife, no reported sightings in response to Bone's oblique enquiries.

By the time they reached the Wellington Arms Alex, with more drinks inside him than was good for him on a near-empty stomach, had quite forgotten what the man they were seeking looked like, or indeed who they were seeking at all, and why. Of one thing he was tolerably sure, and that was that he had never set foot in this pub before. It was on the corner of Shaftesbury Avenue and Rupert Place, and he could remember, during the course of last night's epic pub crawl, James Flood advising him that no true Sohoite ever set foot in Shaftesbury Avenue except to cross over into Chinatown. He had said it several times.

Then Kim Grizzard wasn't a true Sohoite, for he was lolling at the marble and mahogany bar of this Shaftesbury Avenue gin palace, nursing a large Scotch and showing an easy familiarity with the place. 'Tell Mr O'Reilly it's Kim Grizzard,' he was instructing the barman in thick tones. 'I'll only keep him a moment.'

'But he's upstairs having his lunch, Mr Grizzard.'

'He can drink that later. Tell him it's urgent. Go on, be a good chap.'

As the barman reluctantly took himself up the stairs, Alex looked around for the gents', and was at once struck with the sensation of *déjà vu*. For if he had not been in this pub before he had certainly seen that heavy varnished door before, with the inscription 'Gentlemen' in black Gothic lettering.

And as he passed through the door it all came back. The Post-it slip on the urinal wall. 'Does anyone ever see Big John who used to come in here and Muriel's? He liked a drink and a fight.' To which the PS 'RIP' had been added. And now there was a further addendum: 'Balls. He is on remand in Brixton for GBH.'

Alex came out of the gents' and looked as casually as he could towards the corner table by the Shaftesbury

Avenue entrance to the pub. Yes, he had a result. Dapper, middle-aged, clerkish, sipping half a Guinness and reading the latest edition of the *Evening Standard*, which had changed its headline: SOHO MURDER KNIFE FOUND.

He rejoined Detective Sergeant Bone at the bar and rather over-conspiratorially murmured: 'Bloke in that corner near the bogs. Half a Guinness and the *Evening Standard*.'

Without looking round Detective Sergeant Bone glanced up into one of the heavily engraved mirrors that festooned the Victorian pub.

'Sure?'

'Positive.'

'All right, don't look round. Make conversation.'

Quite taken with the role he had been assigned in this little drama, Alex said jauntily, if far too loudly: 'Man U were shite on Saturday, didn't you reckon?'

'Dunno about that, I'm an Arsenal man myself,' said Detective Sergeant Bone with appalling stiltedness, his eyes fixed on the mirror. Alex racked his brains for something conversational to add to the conversation.

Meanwhile Kim Grizzard had positioned himself towards the end of the bar, opposite the caryatid-littered curving staircase down which the landlord could be expected to make his appearance, which he now did. With a napkin tucked into a yellow plaid waistcoat, and bristling handlebar moustaches, he obviously regarded himself as a bit of a character.

'Ah, Master Grizzard himself!' boomed mine host, as he no doubt described himself. 'I was expecting you at breakfast time, not lunch time.'

'Sean! You've found it!' In his relief Kim Grizzard mimed an elaborate heart-attack.

'Found what, Kim?' The landlord winked owlishly down the bar at Detective Sergeant Bone, who was ploddingly discussing with Alex the merits and demerits of Leeds United.

'Come on, Sean, stop pissing me about. Where was it?'

'Right here under the cider barrel, where your young friend left it.' Yeh yeh yeh yeh, it was all coming back now. They had come in through the Shaftesbury Avenue entrance, had the one, had a slash, and gone out through the Rupert Place door. Completely forgetting about the script. And that little bloke was sitting over there fiddling with his Swiss Army knife. So why didn't Detective Sergeant Bone go over and nick him, then? What was he waiting for? To finish his drink, most likely.

'He's no friend of mine, Sean. So what have you done with it?'

'Well, now.' The landlord paused weightily. Alex, listening, felt almost sorry for Kim Grizzard, saddled as he was with the publican's determination to wring the last drop of juice out of the situation.

'Yes, well, get on with it, Sean. Is the script safe, that's all I want to know?'

'It's in the safest place you could ever dream of, Kim. I took one look at your title, *Freeze When You Say That,* and I thought, There's only one home for this till he comes in for it.' The landlord paused drolly for effect, his tongue plunged into his cheek.

'Oh, fucking come on, for Christ's sake!'

'Well, where would you put a book with a title like that, if you wanted to keep it safe and sound?' asked the landlord, in the slightly sulky tones of one whose joke is being spoiled.

'All right, Sean, I've got it. Come in, Kim. The deep freeze, right?'

The landlord allowed himself a beam of self-congratulation. 'Mind you, I'm not saying it won't be smelling strongly of lasagne or fish pie by the time you've got it thawed out.'

He went over to the deep freeze in a cubbyhole behind the bar. A cloud of dry ice rose as he slid back the lid and extracted what looked like, and in fact was, a solid block of A4 ice about two and a half inches thick. 'Jesus, haven't I been saying this thing's turned up too high?' exclaimed the landlord as he plonked the ice parcel down on the bar counter like a frozen chicken. Through it, as in a distorting mirror, could be seen Kim's wilting title page. *Freeze When You Say That*, a novel by Kim Grizzard, in a typescript that waved and curled as if it were under water, as of course it would be once it had thawed.

Kim didn't speak, probably couldn't speak, but simply sank on to a bar stool and began to caress the A4 ice pack until his palms grew moist.

Having extracted all the entertainment value he could out of the frozen manuscript, the landlord, twirling his moustaches, moved along the bar to ingratiate himself with Detective Sergeant Bone.

'Morning, Sergeant Bone, and how's Sergeant Bone? Haven't seen the good Inspector Wills of late. Do give him my—'

Even Alex could see that he might just as well have held up an illuminated sign flashing 'Police'.

'Shut it!' snarled the detective sergeant.

Too late. Alex heard the scrape of a bar stool and, turning – he guessed he was now allowed to do so – was in time to see the stool hurtled across the floor and Bone's quarry diving through swing doors, with Detective Sergeant Bone sprawling over the obstacle as he headed in pursuit.

No one had ever accused Alex of thinking on his feet so it was probably instinct rather than quick intelligence that made him figure out that instead of dashing up Shaftesbury Avenue, where his flight would be impeded by the drifting crowds and thick traffic, the fugitive might just turn immediately right into Rupert Place along the side of the pub and try to lose himself in the maze of quiet little streets.

Without much idea of what he meant to do with it, except a feeling that he ought to be armed, Alex grabbed the ice-bound copy of *Freeze When You Say That* from the bar counter and, with Grizzard's protesting oaths ringing in his ears, crashed through the Rupert Place door of the pub in time to see the wanted man haring across the street.

With a skill he did not know he possessed, he skimmed the frozen manuscript across the Tarmac like an ice-hockey puck. Following the camber of the street, it curled around the man's feet. Startled, he stumbled, slithered and went flat on his face.

Charging up behind him, Detective Sergeant Bone jumped heavily on his back. 'Well done, Alex,' he panted. 'Though mark you, if it turns out we've got the wrong bloke, he can probably do you for compensation. In fact,' he added as he struggled with his handcuffs, 'the way things are going these days, he'll most likely sue you in any case.'

12

James Flood had got the whole story from Detective Inspector Wills, although to his great disgust all he could use of it was that a man was being held.

The man was Christine's divorced father, who ran a small jewellery repair business in Hatton Garden, where he also lived in a tiny flat. He had always entertained hopes that his only son Christopher would join him in the family business, and could never figure out why he had opted to take an accountancy course instead. Now he understood: it was so that Christopher, Christine, could lead two lives, as separate from one another as could be.

This was something that Colin Yardley, as his name was, himself well understood. He was, Detective Inspector Wills had established, no stranger to Soho. It was his habit to visit a certain establishment in Brewer Place once a week with the object of having himself tied to a bed and tickled with feathers. It was his inability to interest Mrs Yardley, Christine's mother, in this bizarre pursuit that had led to the breakdown of his marriage; and it was on one of his regular visits to Soho to indulge in his unusual hobby that he had first seen his son dressed up as a young woman.

Detective Inspector Wills could not entirely understand why a man with a depraved taste for bondage games should react with such disgust at a son who turned out to be a transvestite. It was, to his mind, a classic case of the pot calling the kettle black. But with that smattering of psychological insight that rubs off on most long-term Soho dwellers, the inspector divined that Colin Yardley had transferred disgust at his own sexual antics to disgust at Christine's. Some such Freudian bollox anyway, he told Detective Sergeant Bone.

Or maybe it was simple shock. In his son's youth he had surprised him one afternoon in the parental bedroom dressing up in his mother's underclothes, and had given him such a good hiding that he considered him cured. It was therefore with dismay that he had recognised Christopher as Christine, poncing along Old Compton Street in high heels like a Soho brass.

At all events, he had kept cautious track of Christine over the weeks, familiarising himself with her movements, and finally accosting her in Greek Street where they had sat at an outdoor café table with untouched thimbles of coffee and, in his words, 'had it out'.

Colin Yardley found his son unrepentant and unashamed, which made him angrier and even more disgusted than he was already. But it was when Christine, herself angry, hinted darkly that she had no doubt her father had secrets he wouldn't want the world to know about that her fate was sealed. Did she know about his visits to Brewer Place? This was Soho, where everyone knew everything.

Christine's father fondled the Swiss Army knife he always kept in his jacket pocket for carrying out small jewellery repairs. As Christine flounced off he rose and took himself down to the Wellington Arms for a much-needed half of Guinness. He knew what time she would be arriving at the Transylvania Club and what time she would be leaving. He knew where she lived in Hog Court, had often stood below her curtained window until the light went out. He was trembling with rage. It was time to get it over with.

Meeting James Flood in the French House, where he was magnanimously tossing little gobbets of intelligence to envious fellow reporters, Alex found the packed pub seething with the news. Christine had been a popular figure and there was universal satisfaction at the early arrest. Inevitably there was someone who had known her father: that weirdo who used the Wellington Arms. Drank halves of Guinness. Alex reflected that if there was ever anybody he wanted to murder – Selby, as it might be – he would commit the crime well away from Soho. The two flymen instigated a debate on the need for the return of capital punishment.

'Can't understand why he didn't do a runner, though,' said the first flyman.

'Nowhere to run to, and anyway he's not the running type,' said James knowledgeably. 'Besides, he wanted to stay around long enough to be sure she was buried as his son and not in a dress and fishnet stockings.'

While a *Daily Express* man tried to tease more information out of James, Alex made conversation with the two flymen. 'Wonder if that old Else knows about Christine's dad being taken in. I mean, considering it was Else who found her.' He had a vague notion that this gave her proprietorial rights in the case.

'Why don't you ask her?' suggested the first flyman. 'No time like the present.'

'But she can't be in here, can she? I thought she'd be barred.'

'Oh, she is,' said the second flyman. 'But they let her drink out in the street. They pass her a glass through the window.'

205

The first flyman edged his way across to the open window. There was a throng of drinkers on the pavement but, immediately below the window, one small empty patch that was occupied only by a little pool of water.

'She's been,' reported the first flyman. 'But she's gone, God bless her.'

'Gone? Who's gone, God bless her?'

This, in commanding, bossy tones, was from the small, sharp-featured woman who had just entered the French – now where had Alex seen her before, oh yes, woman that ran that blurry restaurant, Baldini's was it called, who'd refused to serve him a steak and chips even though he was blurry starving? Her.

'Who are you saying has gone?' repeated Mrs Powolny. She spoke in the excited, breathless voice of one who has important tidings, and doesn't want her thunder stolen.

'Old Else,' said the first flyman.

'Oh. Then you're not talking about Mabel?'

'Which Mabel? Mabel who?'

'Mabel of the New Kismet. She's gone.'

'Gone where?'

'Dead. Drowned.'

Someone persuaded Mrs Powolny to start at the beginning. Very well. She had just come up from Brighton, where she had been flat-hunting. Although this was by the way, she had put a deposit on a very nice second-floor apartment in Brunswick Square, overlooking the sea. Brunswick Square was, of course, more in Hove, actually. It was now no secret that she had sold the lease of the restaurant and would be retiring, and awkward customers such as Mr Brendan Barton could henceforth go and whistle. She couldn't see Starbucks putting up with that kind of behaviour.

The bar manager suggested civilly that Mrs Powolny might care to get on with it. This she was happy to do, since the news was exclusive to her and in the hubbub it had not properly sunk in.

On her way back towards the station from Brunswick Square, she had walked along the front with the intention of having a bar snack at the Metropole Hotel, or perhaps the Grand. She had noticed a commotion, a crowd, out on the beach. There was an ambulance, police cars, black and yellow tape. A body had been brought in from the sea. Mabel.

Cervical cancer. Advanced. Inoperable. Mrs Powolny knew all about that but she didn't know of Mabel's determination to drown herself. She had simply strolled along the front, all the way from where that road from the station led down to the pier, then along the promenade to the point by the war memorial where she had calmly walked into the sea and kept on walking, or, as Mrs Powolny supposed, wading.

The curious thing was that masses of people had watched her but no one had tried to stop her. She had walked until she was submerged and then, with the tide coming in, had come back as a body. None of their business, was Mrs Powolny's conclusion.

'Soho by the Sea,' said James Flood softly, making a note.

'Hove, actually,' said Mrs Powolny.

Over the mumblings of shock, disbelief, tribute and sorrow that buzzed around the crowded bar, the pragmatic voice of the first flyman was heard: 'Will they be bringing her back here, at all?'

Mrs Powolny, having imparted her news, seemed to think this of small consideration; but the Soho pub archivist was present and he knew: 'Got to, by law. She lived here, didn't she? There'll have to be an inquest but after that they have to bring her back here. Funeral at St Patrick's, Soho Square. She was a Catholic, believe it or not.'

'In that case,' said the first flyman, 'we'll give her an even better send-off than we gave Old Jakie.'

'Only this time,' said the second flyman, 'we'll do it properly. We'll take her round every pub and club in Soho. All except where she'd barred the guvnors from the New Kismet. She knew them all.'

'But not the wine bars,' said the first flyman. 'She couldn't be doing with wine bars.'

'She'll be missed,' said the second flyman.

'She will,' said the first flyman. 'Wonder who'll get the New Kismet?'

And that would be that. Mabel would be relegated to a shrinking, distorted collection of anecdotes, and gradually forgotten. Alex could not claim to be saddened – he didn't do sad. But a gloom had crept over him. First Christine and now Mabel. Couldn't claim to know either of them, really, but what got to him was the realisation that behind all the froth and flamboyance and freak show, these Sohoites had lives same as everybody else. Lives and deaths, ups and downs, cancer, the lot. Prick them, did they not bleed, as Shakespeare had said somewhere in Alex's A levels.

'Come on,' he said to James Flood. 'I'll buy you a last one in the Wellington Arms, then I'm gunna bugger off back to Leeds.' Northern line out to Edgware someone had told him, then hitch a lift up the M1.

But why not a last one here in the French House, which was comfortable enough? Because he had caught the

Soho habit of moving on. Everyone in So-oh was forever going somewhere else.

'I'll be with you in no time,' said James. 'I've got to file this story on Mabel first. Good human stuff – they'll like it. Does anyone know her surname?'

But nobody did.

There was something of a commotion around the Wellington Arms as Alex reached the pub. The doors of the Shaftesbury Avenue corner entrance had been thrown wide open and Alex had to push his way through a knot of spectators who were watching Ellis Hugo Bell of Bell Famous Productions Ltd mounting a camcorder on a tripod in the doorway.

'Dress rehearsal,' Bell explained. 'Snag number one is that these silly sods won't walk on by. They're just standing there like spare parts.'

The handlebar-moustached landlord, who seemed to have taken on the role of Bell's assistant or best boy, stepped out on to the pavement and attempted to chivvy the crowd of onlookers along. 'Come along, ladies and gentlemen, there's nothing to see and you're obstructing my doorway.' Fortunately for Bell, a policeman sauntering past took the same view, and the bystanders suffered themselves to be moved on.

'This is just a dry run,' continued Bell, fiddling with his camcorder. 'I haven't decided yet whether to shoot here or in the doorway of the New Kismet Club.'

'Here,' said the landlord firmly. 'We get a better class of passers-by.'

The equipment having been set up to Bell's satisfaction he turned back to Alex: 'Now. I seem to recall your describing the whole idea of *Walk On By* as shite. I'm going to ask you to squint into this for a couple of minutes and if you're not absolutely captivated I might even buy you a drink.'

As Bell switched on the camcorder Alex reluctantly peered into the little monitor screen or viewfinder or whatever the fookin thing called itself. So there were people walking past the doorway, so what? Bloke carrying a big parcel. Another bloke, carrying bugger all. Another bloke. Woman with a posh carrier-bag, string handles. Coupler office girl types, why weren't they at work? A nun, who paused, and seemed for a moment as if she were set on outstaring the camcorder. A traffic warden who looked wistfully at the machine as if he would like to slap a ticket on it.

'Well?' asked Bell after two or three minutes.

'It's only an opinion,' volunteered Alex, 'but I've been more on the edge of my seat watching grass grow.' An opinion he had once passed on the efforts of a member of the Leeds Metro Film Society, so he had it well polished by now.

Scowling, Bell said: 'Get out of the way, you ignoramus. You've got no soul.'

'You owe me a drink.'

'Buy your own fucking drink. Move.'

'No,' said Alex sharply. 'Wait a minute. Hang on.'

Into view had swarmed a chattering bevy of American girlie students they looked like, with big tight-trousered bums and chipmunk faces. And in their midst was being swept along a giggling Len Gates, glasses askew, forehead shiny, gait unsteady. Now this really was funny. It was one for the lads. After a morning on the free whisky at the New Kismet, Len was what Alex would have called totally out of his skull. Legless. Rat-arsed.

'This is better,' he conceded.

'What did I tell you?' crowed Bell triumphantly. 'All human life is there. So I don't owe you a drink, in fact I'd say you owe me one.'

Eyes fixed on the tiny monitor screen, Alex was concentrating on the figure fetching up the rear of the mob of students, chatting on her mobile. While tight-trousered like theirs, this was not an American bum, it was an English bum, in fact an authentic Leeds bum, low-slung, a duck's arse of an arse. He would recognise it a mile off.

Christ on crutches, it was her.

This time it really was. It was Selby.

As she edged past the pack of American students, Alex, calling her name, charged after her – or tried to, but found himself impeded by the camera tripod. His foot entangled in the thing, he shook it free, and down crashed camcorder and tripod as he ran out of the pub, with the landlord observing to a gaping Ellis Hugo Bell: 'Clumsy young man, that. I've noticed it. I've a mind to bar him.'

Out in Shaftesbury Avenue the swaying Len Gates had abruptly brought his flock to a halt at the corner of Wardour Street. 'Now, ladies, this what known as Wardle Street, I beg its pardon, Wardour Street, where many of the great film companies have their officers. Now Wardle Street, laze gennelmen, as you were, no gennelmen present, Warble Street is named after Sir Henry Oxenden, no it isn't, named after Sir Edward Wardour . . .'

Muttering ''Scuse me, 'scuse me!' when what he really wanted to exclaim was, 'Get outer my fookin way!', Alex barged through the swarm of American students, leaving them protesting and addressing him as 'Sir!' in aggrieved tones.

No sign of Selby. No sign of that duck's-arse bum. Lost already. She could have gone up Wardour Street, down

Wardour Street, along Shaftesbury Avenue, across to Dean Street, in any one of half a dozen opposite directions.

Alex shuttled aimlessly this way and that. It was useless. There were six Selbys around every corner.

But wait. Her mobile. She was speaking on her mobile. With any luck at all, she would keep it activated after finishing her call. She wouldn't be expecting him to ring at this timer day, anyway. Night was the time for not being able to get in touch with Selby.

He would go back to the Wellington Arms, have a quiet jar with James Flood if he was there, a farewell drink with Ellis Hugo Bell even, and call Selby from his own mobile every ten minutes. All right, then, five. Worth a try, wasn't it?

His own mobile – now where the fook was it? Left it in the pub? Hadn't used it in the pub. Hadn't used it since—

It was in the upstairs stockroom of Stephan Dance's porn emporium, that's where it was. He had made one last effort to get through to Selby before trying to get some kip, and he had put the mobile on a shelfer mucky books because it was digging into his thigh.

Nothing for it but to go back for it, then. Risky, but the chance of talking to Selby was worth a risk. With some difficulty he found his way to Compton's Yard. The white Roller was not parked outside Eve's Erotica but that did not signify: its owner could have left it in a car stack. But he had three other establishments in Soho, so Alex had learned, so there was a three to one chance that he was not at present in the Compton's Yard one. Or he could be finishing a late lunch. Or he could be out on the piss with Brendan Barton. On the designer water, rather, far as he was concerned – sinister, that. Or he could be staring out at Alex through the blurry window.

Did he really want to speak to Selby? What had he got to say to her, anyway? That starting tomorrow it was all going to be different? He could hear her saying, sarky little cow that she was, 'You mean starting from tomorrow it'll all be the same.'

But he wanted that mobile back, come what may. They cost good money, mobiles did, and by the time he got back to Leeds Selby wouldn't be the only one he wanted to talk to on it, not by a long chalk.

He made his way around the derelict building next to Stephan Dance's porn shop and into the narrow alley. He pushed, as, what was the bugger's name again? Barry Chilton had pushed the middle of the five railway sleepers guarding the doorway, which obligingly swung ajar. He picked his way across the joists that were all that was left of the floor, and up the rickety stairs.

They creaked. He hadn't noticed that on his earlier visit. What he had noticed was a faint smell of gas. Now it seemed stronger. Faulty pipes, most likely. There was a lot that stank in So-oh, because the buggers were too stingy to get things fixed, or their landlords were.

He opened the padlocked metal fire door without any trouble and found himself in Stephan Dance's stockroom. The mobile would be on that shelf there, on topper that piler mags. Grab it and scarper. Shite. The floor creaked even worse than the stairs.

So where was that blurry mobile? Was he sure that was the right shelf?

'No messages,' said Stephan Dance, stepping out from behind a stack of packing cases. He was toying with Alex's mobile, throwing it up and catching it as if playing himself as a screen villain.

'I suppose that bearded Brummie toerag showed you

how to get in,' Dance went on. 'Last time he was found up here he had to be given a spank. Seems he's looking for another one.'

'I thought he had permission,' said Alex lamely.

'I shouldn't think you did, son. But seeing as you're here, there's a small matter of fifty quid.'

'I saw Brendan Barton this morning and he didn't seem all that fussed about it.' What the thump had it to do with this bugger, anyway? Was he the Soho debt collector, or what?

'No, he wouldn't be, but y'see, son, you don't owe it to Brendan, you owe it to me.'

'No, I owe it to Brendan. He gave me the money.'

'He gave you money that wasn't his to give. You owe Brendan, but Brendan owes me. So cutting out the middleman, I want fifty quid from you before you leave this room.'

His mouth dry, Alex said: 'I haven't got it.'

'Oh dear me.'

Christ, he was getting into real trouble here. Serious Soho trouble, he had read about it. 'You can take my mobile if you like.'

'I already have a mobile.'

'Or my watch. It's quite a good one.' It was, too. Chrissy prezzie from Selby.

'I've got six watches.'

There was an awkward pause. Dance seemed to be waiting for Alex to make the next move. He didn't know what to say next. Offer to send the money on? Very likely. 'So what do you want to do, then?' he asked.

'Do?' repeated Dance in amused puzzlement. 'I don't do things, son, not in my position. I have things done for me. That's what staff are for. Don't go away, will you?'

Alex couldn't have moved even if he'd dared to. He was petrified. Dance crossed to a doorway leading to the staircase, where there was an ancient bellpush. He pressed it, and sparks flew from it as it buzzed on the floor below. More faulty equipment. And there was still that strong smell of gas. It was a wonder that Stephan Dance hadn't noticed it.

Then, before the explosion, it was as though the air caught fire, in a series of brilliant cumulus clouds across the room. And ever after, Alex could never remember whether it was as he went under or as he came round that he thought: This must be what it's like to be dead.

The smell of gas was replaced by the smell of spearmint. Selby. She was forever chewing gum. They had had rows about it, over her not taking it out of her mouth when they were snogging.

What surprised Alex the most, upon opening his eyes, was that he was not in the least surprised to see Selby standing over his bed in some kind of trouser suit arrangement that at once identified her as a nursing orderly. He would be in Leeds General Infirmary, then. How the fook had he got here?

'No – University College Hospital, Gower Street,' corrected Selby.

'So what are you doing here?'

'I work here. Casualty.'

'And what am I doing here? It wasn't wunner them fookin nail bombs, was it?'

'Gas explosion. What you were doing in a place like that we won't ask. When in Soho, I suppose.'

'I had a reason. I'll tell you, one day.'

'I'm sure you will, when you think it up. But the man you were with – was he a friend of yours?'

'Creditor. Why?'

'He's dead, I'm afraid. He got the full blast.'

'What about me? Am I dead?'

'You'll live. Slight concussion and singed eyebrows, otherwise they wouldn't have left you to my tender mercies,' smiled Selby. She'd had her hair cut. She was looking really good. Lost some weight too. Got ridder that puppy fat. 'I've just got to have a word with the doctor. Shan't be a tick.'

It wasn't a bed he was lying on, it was one of those stretcher things that they wheeled you about on. He seemed to be in a kind of corridor off the main ward. He had all his clothes on, minus his shirt and jacket. Was he on his way to some department or other, X-ray, maybe, or on his way back? He would soon see.

So that was So-oh done and dusted. He'd scored, had a few laffs, got pissed, made a few mates. Worth a detour. What next?

Selby returned, carrying his jacket and shirt.

'The doctor's given you the OK to leave, if you feel up to it. Oh, and I forgot – a friend of yours called in, a newspaper reporter, while you were out for the count, but she wouldn't let him see you. He left you a note. It's in your inside pocket.'

Alex propped himself up, somewhat groggily, to a sitting position, and took his jacket. The scribbled letter from James Flood was in an envelope together with five twenty-pound notes, bless him.

Glad to hear you'll be all right when you come round. More than can be said for Stephan Dance – he fully intended to burn the place down, according to Benny Wills, but not so spectacularly. The good news is that what with Christine, Mabel and now this, I'm to be given a bonus. Not bad for a first day's work, eh? This is your share. Don't get too pissed. Cheers. Come and see us again soon.

Yes, he would.

Replacing the envelope in his jacket pocket, Alex's fingers touched a piece of pasteboard. The invitation to the Soho Ball which old Else had given him. He drew it out.

Selby had evidently already seen it. 'That's tonight, in case you're wondering. Who are you taking?'

'Nobody. For one thing, I don't have a DJ.'

'There's a Moss Bros in Covent Garden where you can hire one. You'd just catch them open, if you wanted to go.'

'Do you want to go, Selby?'

'I haven't been asked yet. But I finish my shift at seven.'

'All right, so I'm asking.'

'You *shall* go to the ball,' smiled Selby. She kissed him lightly on the forehead. 'I've missed you.'

'Missed you as well. Does this mean we're an item again?'

'Depends. I'm not going back to Leeds, you know,' she said with her customary stubbornness.

'So I'd have to come down here?'

'Why not?'

Good question. Why ever not? He had lived more life in the past twenty-four hours than in the last year.

Course, it wouldn't be like that every day. With Leeds caution he said: 'What if it doesn't work out?'

'What if it doesn't?' shrugged Selby. 'We're young enough. It wouldn't be the end of the world.'

Nor would it, put like that. 'Where are you living?' he asked her.

'Stanmore, at present, in a nurses' hostel.'

Where the fook was Stanmore?

'Fook Stanmore. I'd want to live in So-oh.'

'So would I, when we could afford it.'

Hooked on Soho, then, the pair of them. 'I'll have to think about it,' he said, the native caution returning. 'What would I do down here?'

With a touch of her old impatience Selby said: 'Oh, you'll pick up something. There's always plenty going on in Soho.'

'Yes,' said Alex with a rather secretive smile, reaching for his shirt. 'I've already found that. All right, Sel, I've thought about it.'